FR/
FROM THE
DARKSIDE

JERRY WAYNE THOMAS

outskirts
press

Outskirts Press, Inc.
http://www.outskirtspress.com

ISBN: 978-1-9772-6720-7

Table of Contents

Ginger

Gene, after awakening and gaining his thoughts and soon forgetting what last night's dream was all about, went into the living room to check on his package after yesterday evening's delivery. *I need to make sure what I ordered is what's in the box,* he thought, since it was Saturday and he had the entire day to himself. However, to his surprise, the doll was already out of the box, sitting on the table under the lamp, its head full of long curly red hair cocked to the side with a silly smile and green eyes staring into nowhere.

When he reached the doll and picked the thing up with both hands he was surprised at how light it weighed, because yesterday the box made him to believe it was much heavier. When he glanced around and didn't see the box anywhere, he tried to recall if he ever took the doll out of the box in the first place.

No need to look for the box because it was gone.

If only he would have believed the reviews on eBay.

For some strange reason, he sat the doll down and just stared into its eyes. But that didn't last long—he blinked to get his thoughts back; it was as if the doll somehow had taken over his mind.

For months, Gene was living alone. Since he now had someone else in his home, he decided to give the doll a name. Nothing fancy, but since he made the decision to buy the doll in the first place—which never quite occurred to him as to why a grown-ass man would be online trying to purchase a doll—a name just seemed to be the appropriate thing to do. And since his name started with a G, he felt that's what the doll's name should start with.

Ginger.

Now that the doll had a name, he now needed to find her a hiding place, just for those times when folks came over; he did not want those close to him to have a reason to scream in laughter. After getting back to bed, but not tired after waking just moments ago, he still managed to fall asleep quickly, not tossing and turning the way he normally did at other times. It was ten minutes to eleven. The dream of Ginger using a jackhammer to crush his skull into a bloody heap woke him in a cold damp sweat. The dream did not last long, and he could not recall dreaming of anything else. The air conditioner chilled his body more. Somehow, the doll was lying beside him on the bed, eye-to-eye. He almost fell out of bed from the sight of staring into those pretty green eyes. When he managed to turn his phone to check the time, it was 11:38 a.m., the next day!

If only Gene knew, he slept for over a day.

After showering and throwing on a pair of jean shorts and his favorite NOT TODAY creamed-colored shirt, he ate a toasted blueberry bagel with cream cheese, washing his light breakfast down with a cup of hot coffee.

Now on the porch, his elderly neighbor, Abe, was pruning an array of multicolored flowers and whistling a tune Gene wasn't quite familiar with.

Abe and Gene had been now neighbors for ten years, their houses separated by only twenty yards. Abe was now in the fiftieth year at his residence. Gene always admired how the older man kept flowers in the front of his porch as beautiful as anyone who mastered in plants, and not only that but had nearly six acres of corn growing in the backyard, enough to make some extra income, and didn't seem to be slowing down one bit. Every time he wanted to show Gene how to make a living farming, the younger one always waved a hand of not being interested, but he enjoyed every single tale the older man shared with him about past neighbors, how to get girls, and fixing up a decent meal.

"Good morning, Abe!"

"Good morning? In a few hours it'll be suppertime!"

Early afternoon in June was already sweltering to near ninety with an even higher heat index. Gene didn't realize that when he normally came outside at this time of the year it was much cooler. Time was just slipping away from him the past couple of days. Then he recalled hearing birds chirping when he came out. *Where has the time gone?* he thought. *Thank God I'm off today, or my cell phone would be ringing from the job! I would have to explain to them why I was late.*

Abe was just smiling his same I'm-a-nice-guy smile. "Enjoy the rest of your day, Gene."

It was a good thing Abe said something, because Gene was now just staring into space as if traumatized.

"I will," Gene replied.

"Doesn't look like it now, but it supposed to rain later on this evening. You know, when it gets hot and muggy, rain normally comes later on."

"Thanks, Abe," Gene said, at the same time turning to go back into his house, needing to get his thoughts together. If only he looked at his thin shadow, he could see the sun was now high above in the clear blue sky.

As soon as Gene walked inside his house, Abe looked up at the sky and prayed that this afternoon it would rain, even a little bit.

Gene's three-bedroom, three-bath home had more than enough space for a single man, and even though he had plans to move his long-time girl-friend, Anna, in with him after marriage, the place would still be large enough for both of them.

Anna.

Anna, on the night she threw herself a huge thirty-something birthday party, while also celebrating five years being with Gene, passed out from too much vodka and beer shots. When she awoke with a serious migraine headache the following morning, she found her boyfriend had finished his night by sleeping with her bestie, a woman she has been friends with since high school, lying in bed naked, a filled condom between the both of them. Instead of going to the bathroom to piss, she actually wanted to stand atop both of them and release her bladder with a smile on her face.

Anna, the woman who swore to everyone she knew that Gene would never put his slimy hands on her ever again.

Over the past year, he longed to get her back into his life, and now he was putting together a plan to beg and cry about how sorry he was for what he did and how much he wanted her back.

With two of the bedrooms empty, probably forever, he decided to lay Ginger on the floor in one of them, atop a white towel, and just give the room to her, even though he still had enough sense to know that to be somewhat of a foolish idea, especially for a doll.

The website's reviews warned that the doll had a haunted past. Gene thought that was quite interesting and didn't hesitate to make the purchase, which was under twenty bucks, which made him believe that it was all nonsense about the haunt.

With expedited *and* free shipping, the doll arrived in a long and narrow cardboard box by an unknown shipper in only a day's time, which should have at least given him a warning that something strange was going on. When he arrived home from work that Friday evening, the box was just sitting there, and he didn't get any type of delivery update from eBay.

He didn't even bother to read the reviews, mainly because there were only two, but what was said about the doll was puzzling as to how something so demented could be sold online anyway, even though mostly anything can be bought online nowadays.

If Gene was not so hungry he probably would've opened the box that same night, but after getting situated after a long day's work, he decided to head back out and grab something to eat, which he regretted not doing while already out. By the time he ate and cooled off from the heat outside, he just went into his bedroom, undressed, and starting watching television before falling asleep.

While he slept, the tape that held the box together began to slowly peel away.

By that time, the television was watching Gene.

The cardboard box was now in the trash container in

the back of the house, mysteriously shredded into tiny pieces.

Later that evening Gene was back outside, but not on the porch. He was doing an Abe impersonation of yard work, trying his best to trim a few branches from two waterfall Japanese maples before Abe approached him. The trees were planted three years ago, along with a third one that didn't make it a month later. Gene was only cutting the bottom branches because he wanted the trees to grow in a straight fashion, and without taking the old man's advice, the width of the trees would eventually cause them to not only block the porch area but also grow into each other.

"I see you're out here taking care of some yard work, young man."

"Good afternoon, Abe. I don't want the trees to spread out too wide you know, that's why I should've taken your advice in the first place when I planted them."

"I see."

"You remember the one that died on me?" Gene pointed to the spot where the third tree was planted.

"Oh yeah. I hope you got your money back."

"Didn't even bother. I don't even think I was charged for that one."

"You know, it's always a gamble whenever you buy trees to plant." Abe always found pleasure in spreading knowledge about growing things, since he was a farmer himself. In fact, in the city of Henderson, North Carolina, Abe, in his younger days along with his father, won numerous farming awards and had many other farmers jealous of their green thumbs. "All I look forward to is just getting at least 70 percent of *anything* I plant to grow."

The two men both chuckled loudly.

Gene hoped silently that if he ever lived to be Abe's age, he wouldn't come outside in the heat of June with so much clothing on.

"Well, young man, it's good you're out here at this time. I'm going to head back in and make a pitcher of iced tea. Good for the hot weather."

"Okay, Abe. I may come over in a few to have a glass with you."

"Anytime, Gene. You know my doors are always open."

"Okay, Abe, I will try and see you in a bit."

Gene was about ready to head over to the old man's place sooner than he thought. For the past few weeks, not too much of a cloud shone in the sky, making June feel once again as hot as August. However, today, just like Abe advised him early afternoon, numerous dark clouds had crept up in the sky from out of nowhere. A roar of thunder bellowed in the distance. As a hot gush of wind smacked him in the face, he looked up. The surroundings were darkening. In the distance, sheets of rain were already pouring, and he could only stand still, smile, and admire Mother Nature.

Through his living room window, Ginger peered out at him through the curtains walking to his neighbor's house.

Abe always dedicated a few hours each week to tidying up the yard, which was not just cutting the grass. To him, the older you became in life, the more you needed to stay busy, especially with ample exercise.

He was out just after sunrise, knowing that even though exercise was good for the heart and soul, no one needed to be out in the hot sun, even if you *were* young. With the weather getting hotter each year, he knew that just after sunrise he could not only see what he was doing, but he could wave goodbye to Gene, because Gene always left home for work early in the morning, whether rain or shine.

"Good morning, Abe."

"Gene! Have a marvelous Monday morning at work today, my friend!"

Abe watched as Gene drove down the street, still waving every few seconds, just a friendly gesture.

But later that evening, Abe was outside again. He wanted to see Gene as soon as the young man arrived home from work, because he was quite upset with his neighbor. For one, not telling him that he had a daughter.

And two, for leaving the young girl at home all by

herself, even though this time of the year school was out for the summer break.

Gene's car was visible at nearly the same exact time every weekday, but this time he was coming around the corner at a rather high speed, then slowing considerably down before turning into his driveway.

Abe positioned his shoulders in a somewhat defensive posture, because he thought he knew mostly everything about his neighbor, just like many nosey neighbors do, when they tend to pay attention to what *you're* doing more than sticking to their own business.

As soon as Gene closed the driver's side door, fumbling with not trying to drop what looked like a sandwich in one hand and a six-pack of beer in the other, Abe approached his neighbor.

"This is strange, seeing you out in the heat, Abe."

"Yes, but not as strange as you, my friend."

"What are you talking about, Abe?"

"Don't want to keep you too long, seeing you don't have any plastic bags to hold your goodies."

"Thanks, what seems to be the problem, because it seems as if something is bothering you."

"Something *is* bothering me, Gene."

"Well, spill it out in the open."

"I didn't know you had a daughter! She's so sweet, but I can honestly say, quite strange."

Gene hadn't the slightest idea of what Abe was

referencing about.

"I wanted to offer her candy, but I didn't know if you would approve, you know, since she doesn't know me." After sighing, he continued. "You know, never teach a child to talk to strangers, Gene. I could've been someone with a messed-up mind and tried something."

"Abe, I haven't the slightest idea of what you're talking about. I don't have any kids."

Abe turned to walk toward his house, his arms thrown into the air, and angrily began to stroll in that direction. Before walking inside, he turned back to look at Gene, who was now bending over to pick up what looked like a sandwich. He shook his head in disbelief and walked inside.

Gene was confused by now, because he had no idea about the stuff Ginger did today while he was away from home.

It took a lot for Anna to forgive Gene for what he did with her best friend and allow him to come back into her life. But love can make even the strongest of folks to do things they never imagined doing. Deep down inside she missed him so much, and being with him, even if just for once more, she thought he could fill her lonely void.

That first night of sleeping in his arms, she dreamed of walking hand-in-hand with him through a park that had beautiful lilies, grass that was as green as any grass she had ever seen, and a pond with clear water and ducks swimming in all sorts of directions. They smiled into each other's face while holding hands and skipping in joy to what seemed like forever. It was a field of dreams while she was dreaming.

But the dream abruptly ceased in the middle of the night with excruciating pain, a pain that was more hurtful when she discovered the sexual encounter with her bestie.

"Ouch!" Her scream even startled herself through the dark and silent house.

Gene was sleeping in a light snore, one in which would not really wake a partner up.

"Did you just slap me?" Gene grunted in a sleepy voice.

Now that first night quickly turned into anger, for both of them. Past emotions of hurt and pain resurfaced again.

"You bit me!"

Gene was still in the process of awakening, but that didn't stop him from reaching over to turn on the bedside lamp, his face more confused than angry, his free hand raised high into the air as if to grab the woman he wanted desperately back into his life by the throat.

"What did you just say, Anna?"

"You *bit me*!"

"What in the hell do you mean, I bit you?" Now he really *was* angry, and she could clearly hear the anger in his voice. "I was on my side of the bed, sleeping like a dead log!"

Anna was just as angry as he was. Right now in the same bed that just a few hours ago laughter and fun filled the air, the same ingredients needed to get a couple back together again. Now, these same two people were as mad as a hornet's nest that was being probed by a spiked stick.

She gently turned over in pain and removed her right hand off her buttocks. The bite was deep enough to require stiches, and her panties were soaked with crimson fluid.

When Gene saw what had happened to Anna, he reached out with that same free hand, not to choke her to death, but to gently touch the round and bloody circle. After wiping the spot with his T-shirt and making out the small teeth marks and how red her white panties were, he was as dumbfounded as she was.

"How the hell did that happen?"

"I don't know, Gene, you tell me!"

In the far corner of the bedroom, sitting propped against the wall with her head dangling over her right shoulder sat Ginger. The doll's head was in a position as if it looked broken. The couple fussing atop the bloody sheets of the bed paid no attention to her. Even if they did notice her, there would still be no way two sane people could blame a lifeless doll for what just took place.

Chicken Farm Road was a strange name for a street, mainly because there were no chicken farms anywhere on this road. Well, not currently, but who knows what was going through the city officials minds back in the day when the road got its name. The long and narrow road consisted of many well-kept homes, mostly of the dying middle-class neighborhoods that dominated America up until the 1990s.

Abe and Gene resided at the far end of this road, nearly a hundred yards from the closest homes on the road. If you were not familiar with where they lived, and you drove down the road at a high speed, you could easily miss where they stayed.

Gene jumped at the opportunity to buy his home as soon as he saw the house on Zillow. He really didn't need all the space, but the price of the home was as close to his budget as any other buyer looking to move immediately could ask for. The heart of Henderson had just about enough crime to drive anyone insane. He really enjoyed the quietness and the fact that not too many folks in the city actually knew the home existed.

Abe grew up in a small family—he didn't have any siblings—but his father still managed to hold down two jobs to put food on the table. But his father thought that farming could mean a good source of income, plus he could spend more time at home with his growing son.

When Abe's father passed away when he was only fifteen years old, that next spring he vowed to his mother to carry on the tradition his father created, even if dropping out of school was the only option, which his mother was very upset about, but her house-cleaning gigs would not be enough to raise her son on her own. Plus, they both agreed that the fresh corn tasted way better than the ones in the can.

The only regret he had was not learning how to can the corn. His mother always took care of the canning process. He never really asked her to show him the technique, and she never asked for help; she passed away fifteen years ago. A few months ago, he almost went online to pick up a few pointers, but he never got around to it

With the aid of his giant John Deere tractor, planting was the easy part.

One very important step to never omit when planting corn: a scarecrow must be propped somewhere in the field, normally in the back where there is less visibility, especially one as gigantic as Abe's crop. Not just any scarecrow, but a good, strong, weatherproof one, with a mean face, which is what Abe's father would jokingly say. Two weeks ago, when the corn reached a height of four feet, he went into the garage and pulled out the same scarecrow that had weathered the storm for years now. He regularly changed the clothes of the prop before putting the thing out for the rest of the growing season, to avoid mold buildup.

But on this particular morning, just another routine check that all farmers must do, Abe stood on his front porch, drinking a glass of fresh-squeezed lemonade, stretching his old bones and muscles every so often, enjoying the warmth of the morning, thinking of how he loved this time of the year because it was easier on the body. He surveyed his corn crop to the left side of his house; he didn't see the scarecrow propped atop the wooden stick at the back of the cornfield. Lemonade and ice splattered around his ankles and boots as he dropped the cold glass out of his right hand. His awkward old man stomp out to the cornfield would've made many burst out into laughter, until they realized how pissed off he was at the moment. The scarecrow had never before been invisible from where he always stood on his porch.

By the time Abe reached the back of the cornfield, he was nearly out of breath and beginning to perspire under his armpits after working up a sweat while overclothed in the warm surroundings.

When he saw Gene's doll atop the wooden pole with her small frame—she was much smaller in stature compared to the scarecrow—with her arms stretched out as if to sacrifice the corn crop to some unknown god, he almost had a mental breakdown. In addition, while his scarecrow was mingled to pieces and scattered into all sorts of directions, he didn't know whether to pull out his double-barreled shotgun and shoot Gene in the face when he arrived home from work, or just go ahead and blast the doll into shreds instead.

He screamed to the top of his lungs in anger.

Ginger went running, but she wasn't in fear.

Abe watched the doll run toward her home and couldn't believe his eyes.

Ginger thought of killing Abe before running off, but she had other plans to work on first, back at her new home with Gene.

While Gene was at work having another crazed day of either finding another job, or waiting until the next proposed banking layoff, Abe had managed to calm down and readjust his scarecrow the best way he could with duct tape and a new set of clothes. At the same time, Ginger was propped in one of the windows in the hallway near the back of the house, staring out at a herd of cattle from one of the farmers up the road while the eight animals grazed in the late-morning heat. An array of darkening clouds began to approach out of the south, and the wind was blowing at a speed that was strong enough to sway a surrounding forest of trees back and forth; some of the younger trees were almost tipping over to touch the ground.

Meanwhile, Abe rushed inside from the first few sprinkles of the oncoming storm, the drops feeling warm as they touched his old frame. By the time he made it inside and shut the backdoor, his new distorted-looking scarecrow was gawping at his every stride, and rivulets of moisture were streaming down his windows. Two of the windows in the living room were open to let in some fresh air, but he had to close them because the curtains, nearly blown off their hinges, caused him to freak out.

As the rain poured, Ginger continued to stare out the window. She actually liked when Gene was not at home, because that's when her energy was most powerful, the same as with her previous owners.

In an instant the cows stopped grazing, but they strangely didn't go for shelter from the upcoming storm. Instead, they gathered into a small circle.

An evil smile swept across Ginger's face.

Once the cows gathered, the rain coming down at its heaviest point and the wind blowing sheets of water into all sorts of directions, the animals did something no human had ever seen them do before: they just started mulling around, the power controlling them unbreakable.

Still gazing out the window, Ginger raised either arm as high into the air as she could reach.

At work, eating a sandwich and surfing the internet while at lunch, Gene felt a strange sensation streak up and down his spine.

Across town visiting friends, Anna suddenly recalled her encounter over at Gene's place when her rutted buttock woke her up in pain, the stitches still aching in pain every time she sat down.

Abe went to the back of his house to make sure the that door was shut and securely locked, just in case he dozed off during the storm. But with the presence of seeing Ginger with her arms raised in the air, and that wicked smile on her face, retrieving the shotgun was next on the agenda for him—after standing up straight from falling back onto the washer and dryer, which kept him from hitting the wall or collapsing to the tiled floor.

What Abe didn't see was much more terrorizing than seeing the doll. Out in the field behind him and Gene's houses, the cows had stopped their circular dance. Now they were biting at each other's ears. The blood was washing away from the heavy rain, streaming down toward his and Gene's houses into a long and deep pink puddle.

Inside Gene's home, the voices coming from the doll's mouth were as dark as the pits of hell, not from what she was possessing the animals to do but from noticing the old man staring at her and falling backward. If Abe would've heard those voices, there's no telling what the rest of his life would've been like, but it would not have been a pleasant one.

When the rain finally settled to a drizzle, with the sun blazing behind a clearance in the clouds, Ginger's arms finally resting by her sides, all eight of the cows lay on their sides, the blood now caking around their mouth and ears. They were bleeding to death. The puddle from the rain and blood darkened every second that time passed. Soon, the farmer would have no clue as to know what took place this afternoon to his small dairy business.

Meanwhile, Gene just had the slightest urge to get back home, but he didn't know why the feeling came over him.

Anna was deciding if going back over to Gene's place was such a good idea.

Abe was sitting in a chair cramped between the washer and dryer and the window, shotgun in lap, just wanting *anything* to happen at this point.

Gene was so happy Anna decided to move back in with him. It was not being alone that bothered him because he felt that finding another girlfriend was not in the impossible category, but her body just felt so warm up against his; that was what he missed the most.

For the first time in a while, and despite the strange feeling that came over him at work earlier, he drove home from work with a smile chiseled across his face. He still couldn't come up with an explanation with the bloody mess that happened to her backside, and he probably never would, but the company was beginning to be worth the wait. *Maybe I was alone after all, even though I'm trying not to admit it,* he thought. So, he just kept driving and smiling.

When he pulled into the driveway, the rain had settled to a drizzle, a giant difference from a few hours earlier. He was not expecting to see her car parked; she was supposed to be at her second-shift job. This was the first time her car was at home before his arrival since she had moved back in two weeks ago.

While sitting puzzled inside the car, he became even more puzzled by the large red puddle that had settled between his and Abe's residence. Normally after a strong storm like the one earlier, a puddle would always settle in that very same spot, but it was clear instead of crimson. He looked around the neighborhood for an answer, but there was no one in sight to give him one.

Behind his home in the nearby field, eight cows were looking deflated as warm blood continued to flow from their bodies.

He got out of the car and rushed inside, thinking that maybe he needed to give her a pep talk and fix some hot soup for someone who might be coming down with a fever or some other ill feelings. Since the weather a few weeks earlier was cool and dry, but hot and muggy now, and no telling what the weather in North Carolina would be like in the days to come, he couldn't figure out why was she at home so early from work.

Once inside the house, the quietness was deafening. The only sounds were the ticking of the cheap clock on the wall and the hum of the refrigerator.

"Hey, baby!"

No answer.

After dropping his keys onto the coffee table and laying his briefcase under that same table, he rambled into the kitchen to grab an ice-cold beer out of the refrigerator.

"Bae," he spoke from the kitchen, but still, no answer.

He was not by any means seeking an answer, thinking she was probably sound asleep and not feeling well. Therefore, he rambled again, this time his right foot mashed on Ginger's chest, a soft *whistling* sound from air being compressed out but no sounds of cracks, which would mean the doll would be broken to pieces.

At the bedroom door, almost nearly shut, the same place where he and Anna had spent seemingly not enough nights cuddling together, her panties and bra were dangling from the doorknob. He smiled. When he pushed the door open, that same smile became a look of dread as he glanced over at the bed and saw the woman he swore to begin a better relationship this time around would become his ex-girlfriend once again. Her lifeless body was dangling from the ceiling the same way her panties and bra were dangling from the doorknob, her face pale and looking as if she was scared to death by a ghost, only she was held up high by what looked like an extension cord from the bedroom's sturdy ceiling fan.

He ran into the kitchen as fast as he could, his cold beer, as cold as his girlfriend's body, spilling all over the blue long-sleeve starched dress shirt on his right arm. He began to vomit into the kitchen sink, not thinking that the bathroom adjacent to his bedroom was much closer.

Gene could not understand why Anna wanted to commit suicide, which is the exact story he later told the

Henderson Police Department. None of the authorities believed his story, and they assured him that they would question him further. First, though, he had to settle down, and then plan to meet them downtown at the station.

When the authorities left his home with his girlfriend draped in a white body bag, he poured the beer down the sink and turned around; the authorities noticed he smelled like alcohol, which they planned to questioned first. Ginger was propped under the coffee table right beside Gene's briefcase, her expressionless face gazing out into nowhere. If Gene were in his right state of mind, he would have recalled just a few moments ago almost crushing her to pieces under the weight of his shoe.

Abe saw everything while sitting in his recliner, which he pulled right up to his giant living room window.

In the field behind Gene's house, the neighborhood farmer stood in dismay as his eight cows, with their shrunken and lifeless bodies lying dead on his land.

Gene was so tired that rubbing his sore and puffy eyes didn't help him to stay awake. However, he had a job to do before leaving for work in the morning. This job was very important, because he was now curious to find out what was taking place while he was away from home. He needed to set up everything as soon as possible.

Everything Abe told him about Ginger, to a person with common sense, couldn't possibly be real. *Or could it?* That question bothered him the most, especially with what just happened to Anna, because he knew that she wouldn't just kill herself.

He had bought the mini digital video recorder nearly two years ago, just to record some of life's precious memories. And even though electronics seemed to upgrade every few months, quickly making a purchase prehistoric in a short time frame, this one would still do the trick.

The recording device, after inserting a flash drive and making sure nothing else was recorded on it, was set up in front of his bed, because he would leave Ginger propped up between the two pillows, which always aided him to have a good night's rest. But with the time passing by so quickly he needed to crash, like now.

The next morning, Gene awoke thirty minutes earlier than normal, but he still felt rested. After a quick shower and a tall glass of orange juice, he made sure that everything was in place for the short movie he was about to make; the majority of the footage he thought would probably not be needed. He realized that Abe was nearing eighty, but what the old man had explained to him over the past few weeks about having a daughter and the event inside the cornfield, he still wanted to prove that his neighbor was wrong—and to clear his own thoughts, as well. Because according to Gene, there was no way a lifeless doll could perform the things spoken concerning her, from Abe or anyone else on planet Earth. No freaking way!

While at work, all Gene could think about, other than still wanting another job, was to get home and check the footage on the mini video recorder. He even considered going home for lunch, making a sandwich while drinking a strong soda to wash it all down, and check what may be on the footage right now. The only reason why he didn't was because the job was nine miles away, and traffic at this time would be horrendous. In addition, he considered to himself, once again, that a lifeless doll was in no way capable of doing the things Abe has been shouting at him. Therefore, he decided to grab something to eat from the building's cafeteria and just wait to get home after work.

When he swerved around the curve to get onto the street that led to home, a familiar scene began to unfold *again* up ahead right before his eyes. He could see standing outside in the afternoon heat his neighbor, Abe, and Gene could clearly see even at a distance by the old man's posture that something was wrong, and he was pissed. *Oh my God, what is it now?* Gene thought.

Once Gene parked and got out of his car, the stench of the dead cows was stifling. The smell didn't seem to bother Abe at all.

"You and I need to have a very serious talk, young man!" The old man's roar somehow drowned out the scent of the dead.

With tiredness in his voice from working all day on a

job he disliked so much, he asked his neighbor, "What is it now, Abe?"

Still shouting and quite angry, Abe replied, "Your daughter does not have the right to be outside videotaping me and laughing like a hyena while I'm out doing yard work. I ought to—"

"What?"

"Don't interrupt me, young man! Then, while I was on the toilet, she climbed up to the window somehow and began recording again! I ought to call Social Services and explain to them how you constantly leave such a young girl at home all day by herself unattended! If school was not out for the summer break, *I most definitely would!*"

Gene had no answer, but since Abe mentioned twice something about a video recorder taping, he knew he had to get inside to check the footage.

Abe was stomping home, and once again he was mad as a nest of disturbed hornets, the nearby stench of the dead still seemingly not bothering him at all.

When Gene made it to his own front door, tiny dirt footprints were everywhere. His head stooped in disgust. Now the thought of not checking the video footage at all crossed his mind. Because with yet another incident, he didn't want to believe that Abe was telling the truth all along. But he knew deep down inside that what had to be done had to be done, whether he would like the results or not.

Inside the bedroom, the footprints ended just over the bed. Between the two pillows, Ginger's lifeless body was still propped exactly the way Gene left her before going to work. Plus, the video recorder still flashed the red light that meant the device was still in the recording process. Everything was in place the way he left them, except for the numerous tiny footprints all over the ceiling.

He picked up the small recorder, thinking back on how light it felt in his hands ten years ago. He flipped the three-inch screen upward and turned the recording button to OFF. The stench from outside had crept into his home, but like Abe, Ginger didn't mind one bit. However, when he pressed PLAY, the screen only showed an array of black-and-white fuzziness, as if anything recorded was not loaded onto the camcorder. He yanked the SD card out. For some reason of hope, he blew all over it as if that would help in any way. He inserted the SD card back into its slot, pushed PLAY, but still, the same fuzziness.

Inside the kitchen now, before he knew it, two ice-cold beers were guzzled down his throat, creating a brain freeze. Whether it was the beer or not, he just stood by the kitchen window and just burst out laughing.

However, he suddenly stopped laughing. He could have sworn up until his last breath that he heard the doll laugh too. Or was that the rush of beer down his throat?

After tossing the doll onto the floor to have the bed

all to himself, he lay on his back staring at the tiny foot-prints across the ceiling.

He did the same the next night.

And the next.

And the next.

For the next several nights to be exact.

Until he was awakened in the middle of the night, the small video recorder showing on the three-inch screen Gene tossing and turning in his sleep, in which he could care less how the recording happened. Another clip just after that shown the eight cows on his neighbor's farm running toward the oncoming storm instead of running into the opposite direction, which is actually their natural behavior. In addition, cows are slow movers instead of speedsters, even though Gene didn't know any of that; he also didn't realize the recording equipment wasn't even set up at the time Ginger possessed the animals.

Nevertheless, eventually things seemed to get better. Because Ginger still lay on her side in the same exact spot where he tossed her over a week and a half ago. Plus, he hadn't seen too much of Abe, whether when he arrived home for work, while leaving for work, or the past weekend, which was a breath of fresh air for him.

Right before the upcoming weekend, Gene decided to slow down on his drinking. The bubbling in his stomach became too much, and he didn't want to create another problem by puking everywhere the same way he did when Anna died.

He picked a great night to stop drinking. Good sleeping weather was approaching as a late-evening gush of wind began to blow in every direction. Dark, thick clouds turned the surroundings into blackness. Claps of thunder roared in the distance. He knew that an early July storm would have just as much energy as the on a few weeks ago in the middle of June. The only problem was that while he slept, the heavy downpour soothing inside his ears, every time the thunder roared and the lightning crackled, his body would jerk violently. Because in his dream, Ginger was stabbing him in his chest to the rhythm of the storm, as she was now in full possession of his soul.

When he awoke, the storm still had the same intensity. That was fine except for one thing. Ginger was now propped in the windowsill. A bolt of lightning cast a creepy shadow on the opposite side of the window, which gave Gene one of the most unpleasant feelings he ever had in his entire life, as if the dream wasn't bad enough. The eeriness jolted through his body so fast he ran to the door and was now outside standing in the rain, drenched in a T-shirt and underwear, panting heavily as if he just finished a marathon. He didn't notice the front door mystically shutting behind him as soon as his feet touched the grass; the storm was too loud to hear the door shut. Nevertheless, as of now he had no plans of going back inside his own house until daybreak, which would arrive with the first signs of light out of the eastern horizon around six in the morning, which would be about nine hours from now.

The next morning, Gene finally got to chance to go back inside his own house. His clothes and body were soaked to the point he almost slipped on the tile at the front of the door before stepping onto the carpet. He just stood in the living room, amazed at how quiet his home seemed, not realizing his place has *always* been quiet, especially since Anna was no longer around. Or this was his first time missing her since her death, even though she was never really around in the first place.

After putting on dry summer wear of another T-shirt, jean shorts, and a pair of sandals, he decided that since he was already off for the day and really didn't have any plans, he wanted to do something different. A staycation could happen next time he decided to take time off. He decided on going to the neighborhood park. The last time he visited Fox Pond Park was last year around the same time, to a Fourth of July cookout.

It didn't take him long to get to the park, since he was only five miles away. He noticed that new signs were in place letting visitors know the park closes at 8:30 p.m. sharp, and all those not out by then would be locked in for the night. He glanced at the timer over the dial of the radio channel and noticed that it was already five thirty in the afternoon. He had to also verify the time on his wrist watch *and* on his cell phone. *Where in the heck did all the time go to? I just went back inside this morning, not too long ago!* But Gene never liked to overthink, something his dad taught him years ago to never do. So, he drove slowly through the park, where numerous markers were posted that the maximum speed limit was fifteen miles per hour.

After crossing over speed bump after speed bump, and putting on a fake smile for the few people he drove past every once in a while, he just wanted to park somewhere and get out of the car for a quick leisurely walk. There were numerous large trees shadowing the roads that enticed him, to let him know that a walk in the first week of hot July weather would not be so bad.

He walked past two yellow signs warning him in black letters: SNAKES X-ING, and the other one read, TURTLES X-ING. Both signs were adjacent to a large, two-acre pond. *I'll park here,* he thought. *I'll just circle around the pond, and maybe my head will be back on straight.*

After walking for what seemed like forever, the sunlight not blocked out like it was if he had stayed on the road, Gene came to the realization that the pond was much bigger than what he thought earlier. Now the pond seemed to be tripled in size. He glanced around to be certain he wasn't hallucinating, but he didn't see his car anywhere, which he should have, *or* any other people, which he should have also. It was as if all of a sudden, he had the entire park to himself. He instantly looked at the watch on his left wrist, and the time on his cell phone. The time was already at 6:45 p.m.

As his pace quickened, he almost stepped on a small group of brownish-green turtles, a dozen of them, blending in perfectly with the grass. Remembering one of the signs he saw earlier, he was glad they were turtles and not a snake. What seemed strange to him was that the turtles were so small he first thought they were just a cluster of bugs, maybe beetles, until he keenly bent over and focused his eyes on them.

His heart rate quickened as he began to walk even faster than before. The group of turtles he walked up to this time were much bigger, and much greener in color, the twelve of them the size of one of his hands. As he took a giant step over them, they all snapped at his legs with what looked like two sharp rows of teeth that seemed to him sharp enough to easily tear through his sandals. He made sure to keep his balance as steady as he could, knowing that something bad could happen if he accidently fell to the ground and they were able to crawl atop and around his body.

He knew something was not right. Not because his watch and cell phone displayed that it was now 7:30 p.m., but after picking up his pace again, almost jogging now, he finally got a glimpse of his blue car. But he could only get a glimpse every few seconds because the greenish-colored turtles crawling all over his vehicle were about as large as he was. He could hear their clawed toes scratching at the car's body, the noise sending chills up and down his spine.

The passenger-side door opened.

The time was now 8:05 p.m.

The shadows from the trees stretched long over the park.

Gene's feet seemed to be stuck in quicksand.

No one was visible inside the park.

As the passenger-side door fully opened, the turtles calmly crawled off of Gene's car, not toward the pond, but into a dense wooded area near the back of the park, Gene very timid by their presence. He actually didn't care *where* they crawled to, as long as the creepy-looking creatures were out of his sight.

Gene sprinted to his car as fast as he could, fatigued from fear, drenched from sweat—not like the way when he was out in the rain last night. When he finally managed to move his feet again, he was stopped in his tracks again. The sight of Ginger sitting inside his car was about as unpleasant as seeing the turtles.

To get to the exit of the park, he drove nearly thirty miles an hour, enough to lose his license. The front of the car banged against the concrete while passing over every speed bump. Although his body began to ache from this form of driving, Ginger didn't bulge while sitting beside him in the other seat; she was also not strapped in the seat belt. Or should she had been strapped in a seat belt?

"Oh, great!" Gene yelped, because the steel gate at the entrance to the park was locked shut. When he looked at the sign, with plenty of daylight still overhead, the sign now read: PARK CLOSES AT 8:00 P.M. SHARP. He lay his head atop the steering wheel, not understanding the events currently happening.

A loud squeaking sound caused him to sit back up. The gate to the park, somehow, was opening, slowly. He looked over at the doll's expressionless face to get an agreement on how the gate just opened, after being locked, on its own, but to no avail.

Once Gene passed through the gate, he pressed his right foot gently against the gas pedal, looked through the car's rearview mirror, and saw the loud gate slowly closing. If he would've glanced to his right, he would've seen Ginger staring at him.

Abe had been out either in the cornfield or in front of his house the past few hours. The recent rains and heat had sprouted up all sorts of weeds everywhere, but there was no soil erosion from so much moisture. After mowing the lawn, those two chores were next. He was too occupied with landscaping that he didn't notice his neighbor was away from his residence all day.

With the heat of the day beaming down on him and his heavy clothing, he wondered if going into town to shop for some items for the upcoming Fourth of July holiday would be a way to cool off instead of risking passing out in this early summer heat. Besides, he knew the old Ford pickup truck not only needed a fresh coat of red paint, but a few miles as well to keep everything up and running.

As he drove he noticed about a dozen billboards that read either Fireworks Bonanza! or Light the Sky Fireworks, in which both advertised that they had the best fireworks in the city at the cheapest prices. The thought crossed his mind of celebrating Independence Day as a youngster and being so cheerful every time his father would light up something out of a green Coke bottle. Mother would always yell for him to stand back while his father was engaging in this dangerous activity, but that didn't stop his joy one bit.

By the time he arrived at Food Lion just up the street, he wished that the thought of staying at home had crossed his mind. The parking lot was flooded with cars. It was hard to find a parking spot. But he did manage to cool himself down a bit.

"Hey, Mr. Abe!"

"What's going on there, brother Abe?"

"Haven't seen you in a while, my friend!"

After being greeted by so many folks at the large shopping center, Abe was glad he did come out. Normally he would either be sitting out on his porch, working in the yard, or taking a nap, but this really cheered him up.

By the time he managed to get to checkout, numerous items stuffed in his cart, his knees started bothering him, probably from being in the yard earlier and now walking around shopping without taking a break.

After a few more greetings, which cheered him even more, he was back in his truck and heading home. But before arriving home he decided to stop and get some gas.

Once home, and after unloading the truck with two plastic bags of items to eat and to celebrate the big holiday tomorrow, he decided to fix a glass of ice water, down a couple of pain pills, and just sit on the porch to watch the sun go down and maybe catch a glimpse of a few sparks in the sky from those who would start their celebrations early before turning in for the evening.

It took Abe no time at all to drink the glass of ice water, which aided in the pills relieving his pain so fast. He stretched his legs out while sitting down, feeling so much better than a little over an hour ago.

Within a few minutes, Gene arrived home. Abe was so relaxed in his seat he didn't even notice his neighbor until the driver's side door was slammed shut. Also, Gene didn't notice Abe stretched out on his porch.

Abe finally sat upright as the sun continued to descend as normal down the western horizon. When he rose to go inside he quickly flopped back down into one of his favorite chairs; the other favorite one was the large burgundy recliner in front of his television. The downward plight sent pain up and down his back. Even though the sky was dim but not dark, his mouth gaped open wide enough to almost touch his chest when he saw Ginger smiling at him from the front seat of Gene's blue Toyota Camry.

When Gene arrived back home from the park he felt quite light-headed. He was startled to find the front door slightly ajar, but without care walked inside anyway. He felt that two aspirins were needed right away, washed down with any liquid in sight except for one containing alcohol. The kitchen smelled of rot and decay, as if the trash hadn't been emptied in weeks or all the items in the refrigerator and pantry had suddenly spoiled or both.

Ginger was still outside sitting in the passenger's seat of the car. She twisted her head in a complete 360-degree turn, surveying as much of her surroundings as her small frame could. Her head had turned very slowly, taking nearly five minutes before coming to a complete stop, where her neck just popped back into place.

By the time Ginger's head finished rotating, Gene was already lying down in bed, unaware of what just happened at the park.

He was asleep as soon as his head hit the pillow. The dreams came quickly, the first one reminiscing to when he was playing Little League baseball. He hit the ball so hard on the first pitch that it knocked the pitcher's head completely off, a gush of blood shooting up like a water fountain. Then, Ginger's head replaced the pitcher's head, but the blood continued to flow, even more than before. The bedsheets under him became wrinkled and out of place as Gene began to toss and turn. The dream had lasted for nearly an hour.

Outside, Ginger was finally out of the car and now stood at the entrance to the front door, the surroundings now completely dark. The door swung open freely on its own, and the doll's face shown how pleased she was with that.

Abe didn't see any of this happening, because he was too busy either taking more pills to ease his new back pain, locking his doors, or making sure his shotgun was loaded.

After the first dream, Gene quickly began to dream again. This time it was Ginger, as tall as he was, decked in all black, including her hair and teeth, ushering him toward Abe's front door. The old man's front door was also ajar. Gene stepped right in, the doll giving him a commanding direction to follow as she pointed with her right index finger to go inside Abe's house. Her powers were much stronger in the dream, and Gene was her obeying puppet on this side of the world.

Abe was lying on the same bed in the same bedroom that he and his deceased wife had shared for many years, with many good times and a few bad ones. One thing he and Gene had in common, other than now not believing in one another all of a sudden, they both never slept in any other rooms of their houses except the one shared with the woman they cared for.

Gene continued to creep inside Abe's house until he reached the old man's bedroom.

The doll stood behind him in the dark shadows of the house, unable to be seen in her full black attire.

Abe snored loud enough to wake up a neighbor, except the one standing over him at the moment.

Gene lifted Abe's head with both his hands, cocked the neck forward, and was about to squeeze the life out of the old man.

Three buck shots blasted from Abe's larger-than-life .38 special. This particular gun was one of the heaviest of its kind, and he had to use both hands to avoid being knocked backward after each shot. Abe bought the Cimarron 1890 Remington to just mount on the wall, and this was only the fifth time he used the large handgun since buying it ten years ago; the other four times were to just familiarity using the handgun in the backyard by practicing and getting use to its kick.

"I'll kill both you motherfuckers if you don't get the hell off my property!"

Gene finally awoke from his nightmare, the three loud shots ringing in both his ears. But he had no idea why he had fallen asleep on Abe's front porch.

"Gene," the old man added, his voice almost at the highest tone in his entire life, "what in God's name are

you doing out here asleep on my front porch in the middle of the night! And why the hell were you scratching
on my front door like some maniac! Look at it! All those
scratches!"

As always, Gene had no answer. He couldn't even
remember the two dreams he just had. The coolness of
the concrete chilled one side of his body, as if he were
asleep for quite some time.

"I was in the process of fixing breakfast, heard the
scratching at the door, and came out to find you in a deep
sleep, that thing lying beside you."

Gene was somewhat relieved that Abe was not yelling
so loudly at him, increasing the ringing in his ears.

In Abe's cornfield, as the sun started to ascend in the
eastern horizon for yet another fireworks holiday, a large
group of black crows had gathered together, waiting on
just a bit more sunshine, not ready to attack the vegetative
stage of the green cornstalks, but to peck at his distorted-
looking scarecrow.

Gene just stared up at Abe dumb-founded.

"I almost stepped onto you and shot you mistakenly
for a burglar, but I remembered the T-shirt you wore yesterday at another time in the past."

Gene just glanced down at his sprawled-out body,
aching from sleeping on the hard concrete porch.

"Are you okay, Gene?"

Gene managed to painfully roll over, squishing

Ginger under him.

"Hey, buddy, why are you carrying that doll around with you?"

Gene groaned as he sat up. He picked up the doll by her right arm and began to slowly ambulate to his residence.

Atop an old and rusty fence adjacent to Abe's cornfield, nearly two dozen black crows perched themselves in a single-file formation. They began to sing a deafening chorus of caws that rang throughout the neighborhood. After around three minutes, they changed the chorus to a series of grating coos, rattles, and clicks, which lasted for another two minutes. The surroundings were now light enough to see into every direction. The crows were finally ready to do what they came for, total destruction on Abe's scarecrow.

Abe, after watching his neighbor go inside his house, thought about going around the house to let off a few more rounds but couldn't quite understand what was going on with Gene and that doll.

When Abe finally managed to go inside, and Gene managed to sit on the living room couch just to try and get his thoughts together, somehow Ginger was back inside the blue Toyota, but this time she was sitting behind the steering-wheel.

Many small towns in America literally have nothing to do, no matter what state they are in. One of the main reasons larger cities continue to grow is because small town folks tend to move to a larger city instead of living in what is referred to as the country, or sometimes referred to as the sticks.

But in Eldora, Iowa, there's *something* to do, which is shocking for a city with less than three-thousand residents. A show is regularly on stage at the Grand Theatre 1, children can have a blast at Adventureland Park, a quick visit to Blank Park Zoo, or a night of fun can happen with adults at the Firehouse Saloon and Grill.

Sissy Owens grew up in Eldora and has lived in her hometown for the majority of her entire life. Even though she attended UCLA and lived for four years in the giant metropolis of Los Angeles. Moving back home was always her plan after finishing her degree in biophysics. She wanted to continue the legacy of farming in the state by taking on a very demanding and serious role as an agricultural scientist.

The happiest moment of Sissy's life occurred when her high school beau, Jeff, proposed to her, promising to make her the most cheerful woman on the planet. Even though they were young, she totally believed every word he spilled into her ears. She was head over heels, so excited to tell everyone she was close to. And even though he spent four years in the army while she was away in college, the two settled down and quickly married after they had the chance to move away from home to explore someplace else in the world.

But things drastically changed nine years after marriage. Sissy never in her life wanted to be enemies with anyone. She and Jeff never even had one argument. The entire community, no matter the race, loved her to pieces. Finding out her young daughter may be possessed meant it was time for her to finally become a bother to someone.

Brad Freeman had to take out a restraining-order on the Owenses. Over the past several years he had sold hundreds, if not over a thousand, items online, nearly anything to keep a roof over his head, which he was easily able to accomplish. Therefore, he was not about to be harassed and sued by selling an item to someone in Iowa that he had no idea about. He had received a complaint once, but it was about a customer who didn't receive an item on time, even though the item arrived only one day late. Besides, he only knew family and friends in his home state of Michigan.

Carla Owens turned eight three months ago. For each year on her birthday her mother did the best she could to buy her daughter a doll, to have a collection up until her twelfth birthday, the same practice Sissy's mother had done for her, sort of like a generational thing.

The exorcism performed on Carla just three weeks ago up to now has absolutely done nothing to soothe the child's continuous nightmarish dreams and frightening moments. Whenever the child saw *anyone* whether male or female with reddish-brown hair, she would scream out loud, "Help, Mommy! Molly is about to get me!" When the incident occurred twice in school, the principal overlooking the body of elementary students was sure to warn the authorities.

"No, Officer, there's nothing wrong with my daughter."

"That's not what the school superintendent says, Mrs. Owens."

"I will do my best to ensure everyone that my daughter is just fine."

"Okay, ma'am. But do so before sending the child back to school. The faculty there says your daughter is scaring all the kids."

Pastor Brent Monroe promised the Owenses after speaking to them a day ago that their child would eventually get better. But as of now, the child seemed to be getting worse. Pastor Monroe, Eldora's number one evangelist, was okay with the outbursts at school, but was shocked to hear that at night the Owenses finally had to decide to tie the young girl to the four bedposts, tired of not getting their proper rest. Carla was waking up in the middle of the night, going into her parents' bedroom, and scratching and clawing at the bed sheets. Even though Sissy constantly trimmed Carla's fingernails once these strange events started taking place, they seemed to grow back to extremely longer lengths than before in just a matter of hours. Or was this just a part of the young child still being in a state of possession?

Brad Freeman, along with his attorney, could care less about what was happening to Carla Owens. They both agreed to give the Owenses one final warning to leave Mr. Freeman alone or else they were going to be the ones taking out a lawsuit. Strange enough, it was the second blemish on his nearly perfect seller profile.

Pastor Monroe was now spending nights walking and pacing his living room floor, confused as to why he failed a family for the first time as a minister. He decided it was now best for him to step down as his church's head in the Department of Ministry. There was no way the only exorcism out of nearly sixty he has performed in the last forty years failed, and the reason was because someone was possessed by a...doll? He couldn't muster up the strength to explain to any other pastor in this field of work why things didn't go according to plan.

Gene didn't have a lot of friends at any time of his young life so far, even though he got along with every single person that knew him, which is why he had no one to consult with concerning Ginger.

He later found himself at the H. Leslie Perry Memorial Library in downtown Henderson, not to check out any books, but to do some research on real-life haunted dolls. He could've done all this at home on his laptop, or just pulled up information on his cell phone, but this was a job he knew needed to be done professionally.

Gene was quite surprised at how many dolls over the past sixty years were reported as being possessed, and how many different websites contained information about the subject. The only thing that comforted him was that all the dolls shown were either a part in fictional movies or on late-night television special programs. To his surprise, he recalled watching a few movies about some of the dolls featured on these websites.

But that was not the reason he was at the library. Gene wanted to dig in deeper, to find dolls that were strange and creepy in *real life*. He found a website that contained a list of the most terrifying dolls in America that were not fictional but real. They even had the dolls listed in an order from the fortieth spot, which was the least terrifying, all the way up to number one, which was sure to give anyone on the site the creeps by the end of the thirty-five-minute video.

The first ten dolls had similar characteristics; they either walked the rooms of some gigantic house at night, scared small children if any lived or visited the residence, and two of them were even reported as having the capability to whisper into your ears if someone ever put the dolls up that close for some reason, which to Gene made him feel as if the owners were just as creepy as the dolls themselves.

After watching a quarter of the video and reading so many articles, Gene began to rub at his tired and red eyes. But since it was early afternoon he didn't want to get sleepy just yet.

He sighed and continued to watch the video.

A few unwatched children running around the library distracted him.

One of the librarians walked up from behind, tapped him on the shoulder, and promised that if he needed anything to just wave into her direction. He nearly jumped out of his seat from the surprise visit, his mind locked in on haunted dolls.

The children finally left with an adult woman. While she pulled at the right ear of one of them, the other one was receiving a tongue-lashing that Gene could clearly hear as she escorted the youth out onto the sidewalks.

The same librarian smiled at him as she walked by unexpectedly.

Within a minute, Gene looked around and saw no one else in the library, which was unusual. But he was not about to freak out the way he did at the park. He decided to stretch in his chair and continue to watch the video, all the way to the end, trying to find some type of information related to the situation he was dealing with at home.

Before he knew it, the list of real-life haunted dolls had slipped all the way up to number five. But just like at the park, two hours had receded away and it was now six o'clock.

One thing he noticed was that the last few dolls in the

video were similar in behavior just like the first ten from earlier. They were either located on some far-away spooky island that vacationers could randomly visit at some attraction, or they were bought in clusters with other dolls, which almost forced him to give up altogether, turn the video off, and head back home.

With patience out of nowhere, the video finally made it to number one, which would mean that this one would be considered, at least on this particular website, to be the most real-life haunted doll in the land of the free and the brave. This last story also caught his attention, unlike the other thirty-nine. The story of this particular doll stated that in the midwestern town of Eldora, Iowa, a family claimed a doll possessed their eight-year-old daughter. Then, there was another claim about this same doll by a man in Michigan in a small town named, Frankenmuth. So far, the only thing Gene could make out about this doll was that small-town folks keep buying her on the web, the same as he did himself. Before the segment ended, however, there was a third incident about this same doll nearly forty years ago. To Gene's astonishment, a black-and-white photo of the doll was shown, and even though he could make out the old picture as being that of Ginger, the young girl in Iowa named her Molly, the guy in Michigan was trying to make money on the net, but in the older photo the man named the doll Adrienne, which he said meant, "the dark one."

"I'll be damned," Gene spoke to the computer screen in a soft voice. "I have the most haunted doll in America... living in my house!"

Concerning the case in Iowa, a former pastor going by the name of Brent Monroe was quoted as saying, "Anyone, I mean anyone, knowing the whereabouts of this particular doll should contact me immediately!" Gene had no idea if the number that was posted was still in operation or if the pastor was still alive, but at the moment he had no plans of giving up Ginger, even though he was dumbfounded about everything that had happen since Ginger arrived in that cardboard box just a little over a month ago. *Whatever happened to that cardboard box?* he thought.

The man in Michigan didn't have too much of a story to tell, not even a mention of where he originally got the doll from.

The man who owned the doll forty years ago gave the doll that name because as the announcer gave his perspective on the doll, he stated that in the newspaper article the man tried to drive over fifty miles out of town to ditch the thing. He thought he had ridded his residence of the doll. But then, after about a month he was listening to music in his living room while trying to relax before bed. Just as he was about to go to sleep, a large dark shadow swept over his residence that actually blocked out the street lights in front of his house. An aura of fear shot over his body because he also *felt* the presence of the shadow.

When he finally managed to calm down and get some sleep, Adrienne was lying on her back and staring up at the ceiling as if she were alive like any other human.

Gene decided that after spending over two hours at the library it was time for him to head home. Strangely, as he walked out of the building, thinking about grabbing a juicy steak biscuit from Sunrise Restaurant just across the street, Ginger was no longer on his mind.

Gene arrived home later than expected, mostly from not being able to get his thoughts together after doing research on the doll, something he should have done before the purchase. But just like any other internet shopper, how many people care about what others think about a product they really want to buy?

He sat in his car a few moments. Once his thoughts came back to him he began to contemplate how he must handle Ginger. He knew things needed to be dealt with quickly, because the realization that a doll that could possibly contain an evil spirit was living under the same roof as he was giving him the chills.

To his left he saw the window's curtain move just a bit, as if he were being watched.

The walk to the front door was a slow one.

As he approached the door, he could hear laughter.

Then he could hear the soft throb of footsteps running.

More laughter followed.

Once inside, with no lights on, a glimpse of the sunset outside was enough to see his way through the house. The bright orange sunset silhouetted off of Ginger's reddish hair as she sat on the living room sofa. For the first time since he purchased the doll, his brain finally registered that Ginger, all along, has been moving around on her own, which also gave him a sense to finally believe in all the things Abe had been trying to tell him all along.

The next morning, Gene, his thinking ability as strong as ever, finally realized he has had enough of that stupid doll. What happened at Abe's farm and while the old man was taking care of nature was one thing, but the murder of Anna was a totally different evil game to play.

Once he realized the joke was on him all along for buying the doll on eBay in the first place, he didn't want to sell it or give it back to the owner he bought it from because two things would probably happen: one, the owner wouldn't want the creepy thing back anyway, and two, the doll doesn't need to be in anyone else's hands any longer, to add more footage down the road to the one he saw yesterday at the library.

He decided that the best thing to do was burn Ginger on top the backyard grill, a method that was not spoken of as he watched the video and read the articles of the dolls yesterday. That's why he planned the trip to Family General just up the street earlier this morning, in which he bought charcoal and lighter fluid. Since the doll screwed up his holiday grilling, he felt that he was going to have his *own* holiday fun, just a couple of days late.

Gene thought back to the last time he used the grill, which was around this same time almost five years ago. He smiled at the thought of how he left the food unattended, and not only did it burn to a crisp, but he was lucky the house didn't get burned down to the ground. Most of his coworkers who attended the cookout were not even invited, and some of the others he really didn't care for anyway. The way the food was blackened would be the same exact way he planned on burning Ginger—to a crisp! But this time he wouldn't leave the grill unattended.

When he pulled into the driveway the curtains in the living room were parted the same way they were last evening. They gently closed back together. He knew for a fact that no one was in the house except Ginger, or maybe Anna's dead spirit was somehow floating around. Or both. But he was so enthusiastic that his mind was finally back on track.

He slammed the car door so hard it didn't even shut properly.

The charcoal and lighter fluid were still in the car, because the plan was not to bring them out just yet.

The house was quiet and peaceful as always, but Gene could feel a sense of creepiness as well. With the sun about to set in about two hours, he opened the blinds on every window in the house, because he didn't want to be looking for the doll in the dark. Not since this morning when he noticed Ginger's clothes were *shrinking*, or she was somehow *growing*.

He then switched on the light in the hallway, seeing something strange on the wall near the guest bathroom. Previously there was a spot specifically there with a portrait of his deceased parents. As he got closer, with an ample amount of light he noticed a large amount of Ginger's hair protruding out of a hole where a nail had been placed to hold up the picture frame since he bought the house. The vandalism impressed Gene, especially when he glanced around and didn't see his parents' portrait. *I know this doll cannot cut holes into walls!*

After he banged his fist against the wall in anger, another hole appeared, but he *knew he made this one!* As he made out the doll's tiny footsteps and giggling echoing behind the walls, his next intuition was to go outside to the car and get the charcoal and lighter fluid, but he had to force himself to calm down first, or else this time he may burn the house down for real.

Instead of heading to the car, he began punching and kicking holes into the wall, but he was not doing this in anger. His intention was to try and grab the doll while she was still in hearing distance, but instead, someone grabbed *him* from behind, on top of his right shoulder blade.

"Gosh, Abe!" Gene said while quickly turning around.

"You just scared the living crap out of me!"

"Calm down, Gene." Abe made the statement while at the same time backing away to a safe distance. "I don't know what's going on in here, but I have a great big idea it may be concerning that doll of yours."

"Wow, lucky guess."

They both burst out in laughter, only Gene's was out of nervousness, and Abe's was out of worry.

What shut both of the men up was Ginger laughing as loud as both of the men combined from behind the walls, her voice clear but distant through all the holes.

"That's not—"

"Now, you're the one who needs to calm down," Gene suggested.

But Abe got louder by shouting, "You know that when you're away that thing goes from window to window looking out into nothing, grinning like a Chester Cat!"

"Abe, I finally believe you. I'm okay now. But seriously, you really need to calm down. I am so, so sorry for not believing you before. Okay, buddy?"

"In all my years of living on this earth, I've seen some strange manure. But I have to say, Gene, this tops it all." At least Abe had calmed down a bit in just a short period of time. "There's no way I could convince this to a single warm-bodied soul, Gene."

Gene really wanted Abe to calm down because an

idea just crossed his mind, and he knew he would need the old man's help.

"What are you thinking about, partner? I can see a curious look written all over your face."

Abe had seen this same look on Gene's face a few times actually. Most recently though when he explained to Abe what he planned to do to get Anna back.

Poor Anna.

"I have some lighter fluid on top of a bag of charcoal in the back seat of the car. But first I need to catch—"

"Don't worry," Abe interrupted while rushing to the door. "I'll have that grill fired up in no time!"

"Thanks, Abe, and thanks that you don't feel the need to explain this craziness to anyone else."

Ginger began running and giggling again.

The two men gave each other the same look that said they both needed to get busy with their assigned jobs.

While Abe was outside arranging charcoal atop the grill, Gene finally managed after nearly twenty minutes to snatch the doll by the right ankle, amazed at how swollen the doll's ankles were, which meant she *was* somehow growing. A thought crossed his mind about what the doll could actually be eating, but getting the demonic toy outside for a fresh doll barbeque was more important, whether she was growing or not.

As Gene held a tight grip of Ginger, holding the doll by the ankles, she writhed and cried ten times more than any spoiled brat ever could.

"The flames are as high as ever!" Abe's voice was muffled a bit through the closed kitchen window, but with the blind up, Gene clearly heard him.

Gene marched to the front door, the doll bouncing up and down with every harsh step he took. And even though the doll was just recently running through the walls of his house, Ginger finally became as lifeless as any other doll. Or was she planning a trick to later get away from Gene?

Outside, the flames were so high atop the grill that Gene had to instruct Abe to back the grill a few feet from the house, even though he thought of burning the house to the ground earlier if he was unsuccessful in finding his demonic toy.

With all of their recent strange encounters, Abe was more than happy to snatch the doll out of Gene's grip and lay it on the high-flamed grill. He slammed the lid down so hard he almost knocked the grill over.

"Whoa! Be careful there, buddy!"

"Don't worry, Gene. I wouldn't mess this up for *anything*, I mean *anything*, in this world!"

After a few moments of smelling the doll burning and roasting on the grill, a faint gray smoke emitted into both of the men's nostrils and eyes. They decided that with the heat of the grill and the heat outside it was now time for both of them to go inside, get some cool AC, and slurp up a few cold bottled beers to celebrate this strange situation.

Once they both finished their first beer, Abe nosily asked Gene, "Where did you get that thing from in the first place? Shouldn't you had bought a motorcycle instead?"

"eBay, I saw it on eBay, and the doll was described as being sort of possessed. But I didn't believe any of it, so my hard balls made me buy it."

They both managed a chuckle at the statements, then, after Gene arrived back from the kitchen, they both popped the top to another beer, bumping both bottles together in midair as a sign of cheer.

"I tell you what, that doll was something else. I was so upset one time when you had just left for work, not even five minutes had gone by when I decided to take a stroll a little bit up the street. Something told me to look back, and when I did, that thing was in the window of your bedroom at the back of the house bouncing up and down, lifting up her shirt as she did so."

"You didn't tell me about that one," Gene said with humor, even though he couldn't recall ever seeing Ginger with a skirt on.

Halfway through their second beer, they both began to grab at their arms and legs, Abe dropping his beer on the carpeted floor in a splash of foam, Gene dropping his drink into the sink, the bottle rattling with a loud *clang,* but the glass didn't break. The sensation was beginning to worsen by the second, and both men were spinning and jumping as if someone were pouring pesky lice all over them.

Ginger had left something special inside the bodies of the two men, even though they had no idea what was going on. Only when she tipped the grill over and crawled onto the grassy surface and cooled off about thirty minutes later did the two men feel somewhat relieved. Because what Gene forgot to read in the description before purchasing the doll was that whatever you did to hurt her, you felt the same punishment.

Abe had to rush home once again to get out of this house.

Once the old man was gone, and after Gene surveyed the red bruises all over his arms and legs, he looked out the kitchen window over the sink to see where all the laughing was coming from. He first noticed the grill tipped over. Then, numerous pieces of smoking charcoal darkening the pretty green grass he forgot to cut yesterday. When he saw Ginger lying on her back on the grass, her hair intact but the body and clothing smoking like the charcoal, out of frustration he thought once again of burning the house down and just moving someplace else.

Gene surveyed the house to see if he could find a spot to bang his head into a bloody mess and just die.

The grandfather clock in the living room ticked so loud he almost needed to cover his ears.

The hum of the refrigerator was about as loud as the clock's ticking, but not quite that loud just yet.

The beer bottle rattled in the kitchen sink on its own.

The only thing he could think of doing was just grabbing a seat at the kitchen table and sitting down for a few minutes, to process everything that had just happened. He used both hands to grasp at his ears to lessen the noises as he sat down.

He got up a few minutes later and headed to his bedroom. Inside the bedroom atop the bed, Ginger's grotesque body lay sprawled out, her lifeless body staring out into nowhere. If only Gene could've seen the way her burnt body wobbled through the front door and down the hall to the bedroom, but he was too busy trying to keep noises out of his ears.

Overhead, what sounded like a police chopper roared above for the third time. Gene felt that maybe crime in Henderson had spiked again, with the chopper busy looking for criminals, and he wanted to run out to the front porch, wave them down, and let the officers know the *real* criminal was lying on his bed at this very moment.

The burnt smell of Ginger's plastic body filled the bedroom. The fact that she managed to tip the grill over, crawl over the grass, open the front door, and walk through the house to where she now lay on the bed at this very moment startled Gene. But at the same time, he was also impressed. Not because his doll was unlike any doll he had ever seen. No way. Because the doll belonged to *him*.

Ginger's body was burnt to a crisp; her clothes were also completely destroyed. The only parts of her Gene could make out were her hair and eyes, which he felt should've been destroyed as well.

Then, the inevitable happened. The bedroom light was on, and with the sun still shining bright outside, Gene could see everything clearly as the doll's head snapped to his direction, her pretty green eyes staring a hole right through him. When she reached out her burnt right arm to him, in a taxing motion to touch her, he just stood still, the same way he stood at the park as if lead were in both his feet.

The sound of the chopper overhead stopped.

Gene thought the crime was close to being solved.

Ginger's lips poked out as if she wanted her lips pecked.

A shotgun blast sounded from the direction of Abe's dwelling.

Atop the bed the doll began to expand, including the arm that reached out to Gene a moment ago. The arm resembled a large burnt bone. When the doll's body burst apart, he felt relieved that this somewhat of a nightmare may finally be ending.

Until what happened next became very frightening. These burst body parts first encircled throughout the bedroom, *and* around Gene. Then, all the parts slammed through the bedroom window, and for the next several minutes encircled the entire house. As Gene looked out the bedroom window, he felt his place was nothing short of a haunted circus.

Gene was *still* unable to move.

Ginger's body parts came back through the window the same route they left earlier. The parts landed in a heap atop the bed; the parts showed no signs of being burnt, as they were now back to their original pinkish color.

Gene wondered if Abe shot himself in the head.

The parts then began to vibrate atop the bed for several minutes before finally clinging together into place perfectly, not displaying a single trace of damage. Ginger's frame was unexpectedly double her normal size; her breasts had grown also.

Before dark I need to head back to Family General, Gene thought. *My baby may get the chills if I don't buy some clothes for her. What kind of man do I think I am? No way will I let her stay like this!* He left the house and returned as fast as he could, probably not getting a speeding ticket because apparently the cops must be still trying to sort things out.

After he dressed her, this time the doll reached out to him with *both* arms!

This time, he actually went to her!

The scissoring position was strong and firm.

This is the position Gene found himself in the next morning.

Gene's dream was unlike any other he ever had before in his entire life. To be honest, he'd forgotten being on top of her.

In the dream, he floated to an endless world of overwhelming joy and happiness in great abundance. The ecstasy he felt at the moment had him swimming blissfully as much as he was swimming between Ginger's legs.

Anna was forgotten , her decayed body rotting underneath the house.

Didn't matter if Abe was alive or not.

The full-time job could go to hell.

Gene preferred this emotion more than just being alive.

He didn't care where the photo of his parents now rested.

The holes in the walls in the hallway didn't matter.

He'd finally met his true soul mate.

In the dream, he floated through trees that had soft branches, air that had the smell of a bouquet of fresh flowers that just bloomed, where dangerous bugs and insects didn't bite or sting but applauded him while he floated through the air and cheered him on through his triumphant journey.

As the alarm clock blared throughout the bedroom, the last thing Gene had a care for was wanting to awake.

Gene had a few thoughts before heading off to work: *I wonder if I will ever fall in love again? If I did, would it be with Ginger? She's so much more fun to be with than being with Anna. Now I am so excited to be with someone where there's no fussing, no arguing, no fear of whether or not someone is about to walk out on me, because I don't want to disagree anymore. The only thing to do to make things right is to keep every single person I'm close to out of my business, which means not going out or inviting friends over, because frankly, I don't think anyone will ever understand. As I button my starched shirt and head out the door, I feel so much happier than I've ever felt in my life before. Well, off to work I go.*

For the first time in a while, Gene sat in the passenger side seat of his own car. Since Ginger was still growing, and he constantly had to go clothes shopping for her, it was so easy for her to sit in the driver's seat and see over the steering-wheel. With his new pair of shades on—he was reluctant to buy Ginger a pair because he didn't feel that was a great idea for a new driver—he was overjoyed at how easily she managed to control the car, especially at high speeds around curves. Even though he didn't want violence to increase in his city, in which police officers may be busy looking for the bad guys, he knew if they were ever pulled over, moving to another city would be his only option.

As he took a peek at Ginger, he noticed she was still growing. Her blouse and pants looked to be about to split at the seams. Her ankles were nearly the size of his, almost outgrowing the rest of her body. But he was about to have a fit at buying clothes, because the next trip would be his third in a short period of time.

What bothered him the most was how long her fingernails were growing. As they grew, they curved. They clutched the steering wheel with ease.

The parking lot was empty when they arrived at his job; Gene *always* arrived at work earlier than anyone else, except for the security staff that watched over the building.

"Remember, be here at five this afternoon, and try not to be late this time. Okay?"

Ginger gave no response.

He got out of the car with his briefcase in one hand and a bagged lunch in the other. He then strode to the entrance of the building as jolly as any happy man could ever be.

The building Gene worked in was a giant structure that had much more glass than brick. In fact, the only brick on the structure was near the four entrances surrounding the building. Behind him, as he gazed through the many glass-plated windows of the office building, his car skidded out of the parking lot, barely missing two of the cafeteria workers, who had to be at work early themselves. The car was out of the parking lot in a matter of seconds, the tires squealing loudly, and Gene hoped again that the city's authorities had something else to do until at least Ginger got back home.

After several weeks, Gene finally began to miss Anna. Before her death, he promised himself that if he ever got her back he was going to ask her to marry him. Now, all he did was think about her each and every night before dozing off to sleep. He could even see her lifeless body floating through the house, which was so clear that he could see right through her, and see objects behind her. Sometimes, while Ginger was in the living room and he was lying on the bed in his bedroom, she would float out of nowhere and land on top of his body. She was so real that he could feel sweat dripping off of her weightless frame, and they somehow made love for as long as they had the room to themselves. Her dark hair would shine during intercourse, whether in the daytime or at night.

But after each encounter with Anna, and when he cleared his mind to normal thoughts, the woman he was constantly making love to was not even Anna.

The woman he was in bed with was Ginger.

He missed his neighbor also. The constant talks with Abe were gone now, and that void Gene knew he would never replace because of the father figure the old man was to him. He wished that he could show the old man how he had the walls in the hallway fixed with a new coat of paint. But what Ginger did to him after the failed attempt to burn her on top of the outdoor grill was much worse than what she did to his scarecrow.

He sometimes visited Anna's and Abe's grave sites,

but not with Ginger behind the wheel. He felt guilty by what happened to them both, because it was what he did that ended the life of a great woman and a respectable neighbor. And he knew that as long as he was alive, this was the way he would always feel about the two of them.

One day after visiting the grave sites, Gene had a big surprise when he arrived back home. Ginger was sitting in a chair he didn't recognize. On the wall in back of her, written in what looked like blood, were the words: I'M GLAD YOU'RE HOME, HONEY! Gene didn't even want to think where or who the crimson-colored substance came from. Now he *knew* he should've burned the house to the ground! But with the way the doll's hair sparkled, the same way the hair sparkled on the ghost of Anna, everything was now too complicated to even talk or think about.

All that mattered to him at this point was the doll he purchased nearly three months ago, the same doll he tried to destroy by burning her to death, was now his best friend.

Ants

As the sun began to rise on this late spring morning in May, the surrounding green pastures looked peaceful and undisturbed. The oak trees that were in the back on either side of the pastures looked like the perfect picnic spot for this time of the year. The sky was so blue, undisturbed by any form of clouds.

Debra drove the two-seat red Mercedes sports car through the picturesque scene with her left arm dangling on the driver's side window, occasionally glancing out on her side at the beautiful green scenery. She thought, *How much sweeter the air smells out here from that in the bustling concrete jungle of Chicago.*

After driving about eight miles, she turned the Mercedes onto a dirt road to take a shortcut to make her drive to Bridgetown a bit shorter.

In the passenger seat sat her college roommate of three years, Kim. She said to Debra, "We should make the trip up here more often." She was smiling from ear to ear.

"Same thought here."

"If you're not too busy by the end of this month, maybe we can come back before school starts. This is very relaxing for me."

This part of the landscape had more trees than green pastures, and more dirt than concrete. Debra pressed down on the gas pedal to inch closer to their destination, leaving a trail of dust of about seventy yards behind.

"Will we be doing any camping while we're up here?" Kim asked.

Oh, sure! That's the reason I wanted to come in the first place," Debra replied. "The trunk didn't have much space after our clothes were packed, but I managed to stuff some small camping gear in as well."

"Well, I may stay back at the inn when it's time for that because I have the utmost fear of bugs."

"Oh," Debra said, in a tone as if to say you stay home while I go out and test nature.

They both remained quiet over the next minute or so: the driver thinking about checking into the inn to first relax her aching legs, the passenger wondering if there's a place close by to buy a can of insect repellent. The music wasn't even playing, and the only sound heard was the sports car treading over dirt and small rocks.

"I wonder if any cute guys will be staying here this Memorial Day weekend," Kim said to break the silence.

"Normally there are a few. A fishing tournament

always takes place near the inn at Snowy River Golf Club, which attracts a large of group of rich *and* cute men. And I've heard that there are a couple of hunks employed now at the inn."

They passed a green highway sign, which read in white letters: BRIDGETOWN — 16 MILES, SNOWY RIVER — 18 MILES.

"So, what's up with Brad?" Debra questioned her roommate.

"Well," Kim replied, "sometimes he seems a little too jealous, and you know me, I can't stand a jealous man."

"Plus, you're too young and pretty to be tied down to someone like that. I mean, someone who doesn't trust you."

"Thanks, Deb."

Kim was pretty. Her long brown hair complemented her almond-colored skin and her deep brown eyes. She was a model type at the tender age of seven when her mother pushed her into an audition for a commercial back in Chicago, dancing and singing a riddle to a candy commercial. She was also blessed with a nice set of legs from being on the track team at Chicago State. Even though she was playful with other men, it was just for the sport of it. But Brad thought otherwise.

Debra thought that with Kim's attractions and great personality that her college buddy would probably have to deal with men on the same level as Brad. But she also felt that if Kim was not so lecherous maybe, just maybe, a man could learn to trust and love her.

As Debra turned back to look at the road, she quickly felt irresponsible when the red light flashed on under the gas gauge, an indication that the sports car was very low on gas. She slowed down the pace of the car to try and preserve what gas was left; she was nervous from not seeing a gas station for the last thirty miles, especially on a dirt road.

The dirt road seemed to stretch on forever, and neither girl would know what to do in case the car ran out of gas.

"Oh, shit!" Debra managed to shout.

"Don't tell me we're about to run out of gas." Kim looked at Debra. "When are we going to get back onto a main road, anyway?"

"About a couple of miles. There's a gas station close to the inn, and we're almost there."

"Will we make it?"

"I'm sure we can." But Debra had only seen the light come on once, about two miles from a station a couple of years ago. "Let's just try to relax and stay calm."

They finally arrived at Highway 51 and turned right onto it. About forty feet ahead, a green road sign with white letters read: BRIDGETOWN — 3 MILES, SNOWY RIVER — 5 MILES, CRESTWOOD — 32 MILES.

"Good. We're only three miles away from a station," Debra explained.

Kim only glanced at Debra for a moment and turned back to look down the highway, which was long and deserted, all at the same time. She felt it was like one of those situations when you live on planet Earth with billions of people, but somehow people always tend to feel lonely, even though she was riding with a close friend. Her lips poked out as if to be a little upset about the gas situation.

Another mile or so down the road the next sign on the edge of the highway was green just like the last one, but instead had two small square boxes inside. One was red with yellow letters indicating a fast-food burger joint was at the next exit, and another square box, which was brown with white letters, spelled SUPER GAS at the top and on the bottom TWO EXITS AHEAD.

When they finally reached SUPER GAS, the car ran out of gas, just as they were turning into the parking lot, about twenty feet from the first pump. Another car was on the opposite side of the pump, but the girls could not see the driver.

"Let's go and see if we can get some help to push this thing up to the pump," Debra suggested.

"This place looks dead," Kim exclaimed.

The place *was* dead. The two girls screamed and jumped back as they rounded the gas pump and saw a human skeleton lying on the ground beside the parked car they saw just moments ago. The skeleton looked to be completely erased of all life only a short while ago because a group of flies were hovering over it and buzzing loud enough for both of the girls to hear. The gas pump's nozzle was beside the skeleton, a small amount of the liquid gold escaping and forming a miniature puddle.

"No! Don't go in there!" Debra shouted to Kim as she ran to the front door of the gas station at top speed.

"What do we do now?" Kim was now terrified, her pretty face filled with terror.

"Let's just stay calm," she suggested as she viewed the landscape. Up ahead in the distance a house sat alone between a pair of oak trees, its fresh white coat blending in beautifully with the surrounding green landscape. Debra pointed in that direction. "There! Let's see if someone's home so that we can get some help. My phone does not have any bars."

They decided the best thing to do first was to get their purses out of the Mercedes. Just in case they were unable to make it back to the car; just in case the house wasn't safe.

Terror struck the two girls again as they saw a man in the passenger side of the sports car, holding his body tightly as if he had fear from some previous experience. The man looked puerile and afraid, the look you get when someone or something scares the crap out of you. He looked to be in his late forties. He motioned for the girls to hurry and get inside the car with him, even though it would be difficult in a two-seater.

Debra realized that with all the commotion going on neither of them heard the man enter the car. She knew now that the best thing to do was to not only stay calm but to stay focused.

Inside the car the man, whose name was Kenny, explained to the girls how two days ago the earth came to life and started eating everything that had flesh, alive. He pointed toward the back of the gas station and told the girls that another man was dead back there; the man was too slow to run and try to escape.

The three remained silent for a moment, the only sound being Kim and Kenny breathing with panic and fear. But they both felt safer in the car instead of outside.

"What do you mean the earth came to life?" Debra asked as Kim pushed her up against the driver's side door, trying not to get too close to Kenny.

"Just like I said a second ago," he explained and at the same time was motioning with his hands to best describe the scene. "Huge piles of insects. So many that they sounded like someone was balling up a piece of paper in their hands."

"What type of insects were they?" Debra was curious to know.

"Ants," Kenny said while his breathing was slowing

down a little. "When I heard you two outside I decided to try and make a run for it. Apparently, they have feasted on the entire surroundings because I haven't seen a live person or bug the last couple of days. I've survived on what was in the store, but the majority of that is not healthy for you, even though I'm not complaining at all."

"Are you okay?" Debra asked the frightened man.

"Am I okay? I'm still alive, aren't I? Anything is better than being dead, if you know what I mean."

"Where did the ants come from?" Debra asked.

"A group of scientists brought them all the way from Africa, even though that's not written in stone. They wanted the ants to be used to destroy the numerous bugs that eat up valuable crops every year. But the ants must have kept reproducing. They grow to be so big."

"Is this your gas station?" Debra asked.

"Yes. Well, if I get through this, it won't be anymore. After seeing what happened, I'm going to sell this place and get the hell out of here!"

"Can we pump some gas and head up the road to that house you pointed to, Debra?" Kim asked.

"No need. The house is mine also. I'm going to sell that as well."

Outside, the sun shone high overhead, indicating that it was close to noon. The three of them had been sitting in the Mercedes for about half an hour now. The red car stood out in the bright sunlight as colorful as the sun itself. Sweat began to drip down the faces of all three of them. Neither one was brave enough to get out and pump gas into the car.

Straight ahead in the distance Debra noticed a huge dark mass creeping up over the horizon. But it was moving too fast, she thought, to be a cloud.

"Okay, guys, let's get out and push this car up to the pump, even though we may not have the guts to, so we can get out of here. It's seems that we're just wasting time sitting here in the sun, like sitting ducks, waiting for the horror that will eventually happen if we don't get to moving." Debra was now talking with exasperation.

Now Kenny noticed the dark mass creeping closer and closer toward them as soon as he started to push the car, sweat beading down his face and onto the concrete. His light blue T-shirt was being soaked with sweat as well.

Debra hurried out the car to help him push.

Kim was the designated driver.

The huge dark mass was still inching closer to live flesh.

Kenny felt as if he would pass out.

Debra finally began to feel fearful.

Kim looked over the steering wheel straight ahead with her mouth wide open, her eyes bulging out their sockets.

As Kenny pumped, the dark mass was now only about one hundred yards away. A rattling sound could be heard in the distance. The shape of the mass twisted and turned in an irregular fashion as if distorted.

"Hurry, back in the car!" Kenny yelled. "And make sure that the windows are rolled up as tight as you can get them!"

As soon as everyone jumped into the car and secured the windows as tight as they could go, a slight breeze began to throw ants one by one up against the car's windshield. Every half minute, more and more ants splashed onto the car, and they eventually began to accumulate.

The shape of the dark mass looked like a low-flying rain cloud, except it was thicker.

"We shall all die," Kenny said in a low and scratchy voice.

"No, don't say that!" Kim pronounced in fear.

"Let's all stay calm, all right. So, is this the way they approached the last time, Kenny?" Debra always loved doing her homework.

"Yes. Hopefully they won't be able to get in through the air conditioning unit or the exhaust pipes." Kenny knew what would happen if the ants entered the car.

"Close the vents to the AC!" shouted Kim in her best paranoid voice.

Moments later, what was a clear and sunny day became dark and chilled—from fright—as the mass of ants encircled the entire car. There were many ants that all the occupants of the car could see was the tiny footprints of the insects. They also could hear the tiny footsteps of the ants scrape the car in a low volume of madness. All Debra could do was pray while Kim began to cry and Kenny looked straight ahead in shock. Even though they could see each other—as their eyes adjusted to the darkness—they held on to each other as if they were in a dark tunnel of death. Now Kim didn't mind being close to Kenny.

The car began to wiggle slightly from side to side as millions of ants continued to encircle the sports car. Kim's cries did not silence the sound of the ants.

The three of them were now bunched up together looking out either side of the windows as if this would change the horror they were watching. But this horror was not a movie, because these special effects were live and real.

The car began to get stuffy from a lack of oxygen because the show had been going on for twenty minutes now. If the ants did not move on to another place soon, the occupants of the sports car would not have to worry about being eaten alive; they would just suffocate to death.

Now thirty minutes into the show, the lack of oxygen and the terror of the darkness sent panic inside the Mercedes. Kenny couldn't take it any longer as he pushed the passenger side door open, screaming at the top of his lungs and waving his hands frantically into the air. As he screamed, hundreds of ants went down his throat, causing his voice to babble. Soon he disappeared into the swarm of ants as he was engulfed in a matter of seconds. It took about the same length of time for the remaining army of insects to fill up the inside of the car, covering Debra and Kim in an instant.

Kim did manage to have one last thought: *A can of insect repellent would surely come in handy right now.*

The People of Sleepy Hill

Frog stepped behind the big ancient house and headed toward the backyard farm huts. He enjoyed the heat from the sun, warming the earth after a cool morning start high in the hills. He didn't see his odd-looking cousin walking up from behind, scaring the living daylights out of him, and nearly causing him to drop two large plastic bags inside of two large plastic buckets apiece, full of precisely cut potatoes and tomatoes.

"These creatures are breeding like crazy, aren't they?" the odd-looking cousin asked. He was the same height as Frog, but a little chubbier. "Maybe one day we can all get rich!"

Frog hated the fact that his odd-looking cousin enjoyed sneaking up from behind him at any given moment. It's the main reason why he stopped carrying his .44 Magnum pistol, because after serving in Vietnam, his nerves never quite functioned in an orderly fashion. It was one morning after a previous humid summer afternoon.

That morning the fog was so thick Frog could barely see five feet in front of him. When the cousin jumped out of nowhere, the plastic bags he was carrying dropped to the ground with a loud thump, the contents rolling freely on the dewed grass. The safety on the pistol was the only reason a family disaster did not take place. Every once in a while, he shivers when his mind recalls the events of that morning. But no matter what, he still had the utmost love for everyone in his family.

"Yes," Frog replied dryly. "Maybe one day we can all get rich."

As the two men continued to pace toward the huts, Frog was in no mood for joking. He was so focused his stare could make the hairs rise on the back of your neck. He stood tall and looked sort of awkward while walking, mainly from a grenade explosion back in Vietnam, which was not too devastating for an amputation. His frame was so thin it was a miracle he still had both legs. He was wearing dirty blue jeans and blue sneakers, but he wore a fresh and clean red motorcycle T-shirt.

"I checked on them last night," the odd-looking cousin said, still wearing his dingy attire from the previous two days, but neither his clothing nor body smelled rancid. "I just kept telling myself over and over again early this morning that this was going to be a real gold mine. I want a new car so bad."

Frog paid his cousin no attention, seemingly unaware

of the voice behind him. When he reached the door to the first hut—knowing that one day they would need more space—the rusty hinges on the gate began to squeak loudly, the high-pitch cry vibrating throughout the hills; a few large black birds passed through the air quickly on their wings as if startled. Frog paid no attention to the birds and descended into the first small dwelling.

"I wish I could fly," the odd-looking cousin explained, his wide smile showcasing an array of cavities.

"Shut up, you dork." Frog now seemed to notice what his cousin was blabbering. He then looked around the hut and agreed, "You're right, maybe we can one day become rich."

"I told you so."

"Didn't I tell you to shut up?"

After the lights flickered on, fifteen twenty-gallon aquariums on the left wall of the hut, each one filled with light brown crickets, became silent; they stopped making music, thinking it was time to rest from daybreak. Coincidently, on the other side of the hut, ten more twenty-gallon aquariums were filled with grasshoppers; they began to stir because they thought it was daybreak. This was the gold mine the cousins just recently agreed upon: insects being raised for a low-cost, high-protein food source. In other words, these were the main-course meals for meat at most of the dwellings—including restaurants—in this foggy and strange city known throughout as Sleepy Hill.

The cousins were part of the Waller family, which traces back at least seven generations, expanding nearly two hundred years. Of all the families living in Sleepy Hill, the Wallers were the most hateful and the most feared. To bother or annoy a Waller was known throughout the town as a reason to accept serious bodily harm, which could lead to death. For years, parents enforced a strict rule for their kids not to play or associate with Waller children, *even if you did* sit beside, in front, or behind one in school.

"Everything looks to be okay in here," Frog noted. "Let's go check on the other huts."

"Well said, Cousin."

Mostly all the people of Sleepy Hill had a change of diet during the depression in the mid-thirties. Now, with the economy struggling again, going back to a lifestyle of saving would be easy to become accustomed to. Also, times were so hard in these rural parts that nearly 80 percent of the town's residents were forced to eat whatever they could find.

The Waller family was one of the first families to consume insects years ago. Unlike other families, they continued to eat them, gaining a stronghold in this area of food consumption. This enabled them to most recently take advantage of the townspeople's hunger pains. And with seven huts full to the max with protein, new competition would without a doubt have to take a back seat in this line of business.

Frog recently became very aggressive toward the family business while reading a past issue of *Time* magazine. The magazine was quick to point out that insects, most notably crickets, would one day end up on grocery store shelves everywhere across the US as a new, better option for protein consumption. The magazine also noted that raising insects would be a lot cheaper than farming cows and pigs, especially since the latter two require large amounts of water and feed to produce a healthy product. And not only do the bugs produce an eco-friendly source of protein, but the low cost to raise them would help benefit low-income nations around the globe. The magazine finished the article strongly by adding two key points: now nearly one-fourth of the earth's population already consume insects as a major source of protein; and two, cricket flour—produced by slow-roasting the bugs and grinding them into a fine powder—can blend into any type of recipe that normally uses regular flour without mouths knowing the difference in a blindfold taste test. So, Frog knew that whoever gets the early jump on consumers will run this new complete diet consisting of B vitamins and amino acids.

One distinct characteristic all of the original residents of Sleepy Hill had in common was the presence of luggage under their eyes, especially those who were now elderly, and even children once they reached their teenage years. This normal appearance is what created the name of the city, Sleepy Hill, because every day you dealt with cool nights and numerous cloudy days, both perfect conditions for occasionally lying in bed.

Thirty minutes later all seven huts were checked. The contents of large plastic bags were distributed in small amounts in every aquarium—the older contents of food were discarded—furthering the healthy advancement of the insects, insuring healthy food for any hungry consumer.

"I don't know why people think this type of food is gross."

"Well," Frog said, "from a sarcastic educational point of view, people will feel that way when they find out that they are eating insects for two reasons only: they have never tried eating them and think of it as gross, or they have tried them and *know* they're gross." He continued by adding, "Once I slipped a few earthworms in a bowl of spaghetti at school years ago. The kid didn't recognize the night crawlers and went on and ate his food. But if I would have told him about the worms, he probably would've puked his guts out."

They both laughed at the scenario while walking back to the house parading in perfect unison, each carrying two large buckets of either of the insects. Their arms were stretched out as straight as arrows from the weight of the food.

Before reaching the steps to the back porch of the house, Frog added, "It's like this, something called mind over matter. If you don't mind, it doesn't matter!"

They both chuckled loudly one last time before entering the house.

As Frog sat both of his buckets down to open the door, he and his cousin jumped into the air, which caused the buckets to tumble, which caused crickets and grasshoppers to jump everywhere, as well. June Stoops, one of the Waller's main customers, came surprisingly up from behind. The cousins didn't even hear his car drive up, mainly because they were too busy lollygagging around.

"June, are you nuts?"

Frog shouted, his mind recalling once again his previous military scares.

"Sorry Frog. I thought you guys saw me pull into the driveway. What was so funny?"

"Don't let them all get away, you two fools!" Frog continued to shout.

"Just because I'm your cousin does not constitute you the right to call me a fool!"

"Yeah, Frog, I'm no fool either," June agreed.

Frog was hysterical at seeing the profits scramble all over the back lawn.

June just shook his head in disbelief.

The odd-looking cousin, named Cockroach, bunny-hopped for insects as if he were trying to get all the goodies at an Easter egg hunt.

June Stoops was a big man. His statue reached six-feet, four-inches tall. His weight was nearly three hundred pounds. The insects were definitely keeping him nice and thick. From the looks of his wife, three sons, and four daughters, they were all having a swell of a time feasting on the insects as well. He rarely changed clothes, and his foul odor was proof of this. His ballooned frame didn't move an inch to assist the cousins.

After catching all the insects, the cousins were tired and sweaty. They both wiped their brows of perspiration and turned their attention to June.

"Oh, I came by to see if I could get about three pounds of crickets and about two pounds of grasshoppers."

"Give me about ten minutes," Frog promised.

Not wanting to seem nosey, he informed the cousins that he would just wait outside until they were finished.

Only six minutes later June had his five pounds of high protein. When June cranked his pickup truck, he waved a joyous goodbye to the Wallers. His joy increased as he looked at his two sacks of insects, marveling at how they protruded and vibrated the sacks, as if trying to escape.

Inside the Waller house, which was big enough for three families, Mother Maxine was scrambling eggs, boiling grits, baking biscuits, and grease-frying two giant handfuls of crickets in a large hot black skillet; the skillet was covered tightly immediately after the crickets were deposited into the hot grease because they always tried to escape as soon as their tiny feet felt the enormous heat.

Three small boys sat at the dining room table in front of empty white plates. They were hungry from the aroma of breakfast. They stared at Mother Maxine as if they wanted her to speed up the cooking process.

Outside, Cockroach was helping Ennis Archer—the Wallers's best customer—bag nearly forty pounds of insects. Like June and the Waller family, he was born, raised, and bred in Sleepy Hill. He needed so much of a fresh and regular supply because he owned Archer's Tavern down on 16th Street near most of the town's office buildings. His establishment was always packed with customers. Unlike June and the Waller family, he always looked spiffy in his Italian suits and custom-made alligator shoes, even when he was picking up his mass quantity of the tavern's principal meal supply. His restaurant had so many recipes for the insects, in which a chalkboard menu was changed regularly. He always drove the latest Jaguar, no matter the cost.

Back inside, the kids were crunching loudly on their breakfast meat. Eggs and grits were splattered against their chin.

The phone rang; it was for Frog. He walked into the kitchen from the hallway. While on the phone a vexatious look covered his face, not toward his family, but from some disturbing news from an anonymous friend:

someone in Sleepy Hill was planning on stealing part of the Wallers's profits by raising their *own* insects.

The meeting was about to adjourn, one called together by Caleb Brunswick. The six men seated and surrounding the solid oak table listened patiently as he spoke, neatly stapled papers lying on the table in front of either one. The agenda focused on not only the success of the apartment leasing part of the business but on launching into the food business by raising insects. The agenda explained how the profits may take a while before coming in. The meeting concluded by asking each business partner to start putting a word out on the streets about this new venture, that a new supplier of insects was ready to emerge in the area.

One thing Caleb was not afraid of was venturing into a new area of business, whether or not the idea was successful. Apartment leasing was paying plenty of money, but he and his associates lost heavily trying to profit into the car washing business. It seemed that not too many people in Sleepy Hill cared enough to get their cars detailed and waxed, or even just simply washed.

After the meeting, Caleb watched a small downtown office building as his six partners drove away. He had the look of satisfaction written all over him. With his hands in either pocket, he jingled keys and change loudly.

But he was not from the area, just moving to Sleepy Hill only seven years ago. He had no idea how aggressive and hateful the current suppliers of insects were. Lumps of cash in various financial institutions made him a go-getter. But soon he would find out that competing with the Waller family will mean big trouble later on down the road.

The time on the antique grandfather clock was 7:30 p.m., which meant that only thirty minutes of daylight remained. As the sun was beginning to set, the coolness of the air returned. The array of many species of birds were about to stop singing. A slight breeze made the leaves on the neighboring trees dance in rhythm.

Frog sat in the living room looking ambiguously. The house was silent here while all the other family members were either playing or watching television in the bedrooms down the hallway, except for Cockroach, who had earlier discussed with his cousin how a few rivals may need to be aggressively taken care of. Soon he would have to switch on a light or just sit in the dark.

A car pulled into the driveway, but it was not a customer. It was Frankie Champion, one of the six business associates of Caleb Brunswick. He looked terrified, because unlike Caleb, he *knew* the Waller family. He was very excited to start working for Brunswick and Associates nearly three years ago, smiling from cheek-to-cheek after seeing a position open in the accounting department in the *Sleepy Hill Times* newspaper. After a phone interview, a set date for an office interview, and a lengthy career in the field, Frankie knew for sure that he had the job. The position also paid him more money than he had ever made before in his entire life. But this mess about getting into the business of raising insects deeply troubled him.

Frog immediately rushed outside.

Frankie thought of just driving off.

Frog stepped right behind Frankie's vehicle.

Frankie hoped that his fear would not be recognizable.

"Well, well, well, seems like someone can't find their way home," Frog jokingly suggested while slowly stepping up to the driver's side window.

"I have to tell you something, Frog."

"Well, spit it out."

As the sun continued to set, the air became cooler. The cool breeze rustled leaves loudly, but a storm was not approaching. Well, at least not one relating to the weather.

"I guess you have heard by now that the company I work for wants to get into the insect business. Now Frog, you know I have the utmost respect for you and your family."

Frog always got a thrill when someone was agonized while in his presence.

All of a sudden, Frankie grew some balls. "I know that you and your family have the market cornered, but this is a free country! And if you or anyone else in your family has a problem with my company's desire to slice a piece of the pie, well, stick your fingers up your nose and eat buggers!"

Frog had to gather himself to hold back the laughter.

Frankie was sweating in his car, despite the surrounding coolness.

While the conversation was being held, Cockroach waited behind a group of large pine trees, almost slipping on the tree's pine needles, dressed in camouflage, plotting in his mind a deadly scheme. No longer in a humorist mood, he now longed to keep the Wallers's choke hold on the food industry in check. In his arms he tightly held a Remington 870 FPS Thumbhole shotgun. Even though most of those who possessed the weapon were getting away from using buckshot, he still enjoyed the heavy kick the shotgun gave his right shoulder blade. The shotgun was so powerful, even at the distance of a football field the slugs could still penetrate deep into any motor vehicle. The shotgun was also automatic on any human target up to a 150-yard distance. Down near his right foot were three cases of Remington 870 slugs, enough ammunition to start a small war. Soon he would look through the shotgun's scope and start pulling the trigger.

Meanwhile, Frankie continued his bold discussion.

Frog glanced at his watch to see how soon he would dismiss this scumbag.

Frankie finally shivered from the evening breeze. He

was totally unaware that his other business partners were about to be ambushed by other Waller family members right at this very moment. He was unaware of his fate as well.

Three minutes later, Frog decided that it was time to dismiss the scumbag.

Frankie skidded through the driveway and onto the road that led to home. He was so disgusted at the fact that Frog had an attitude toward his company's ambitions. He decided that he would never do any type of business with the Waller family. The speedometer read 85 mph. Within a minute, he jumped at the sound of a loud blast.

Frog heard the shotgun blast in the distance.

Cockroach almost fell backward from the explosion.

Frankie skidded onto the banks of the long-stretched road, half of his head escaping outside the driver's side window.

Cockroach almost fell backward again when he pulled the trigger the second time.

The corners of Frog's mouth turned up in an expression of amusement, knowing that the latest of his competition was no longer. One thing he knew about his odd-looking cousin was when a shotgun was in his arms, the target had no chance of survival.

After all the excitement—mainly ambulances and local news reporters—Sleepy Hill was once again enjoying a cool and quiet night.

The next morning, Frog and Cockroach made that same routine walk to check on each hut, giving not one thought to the deadly events from last evening, ensuring that their product was alive and healthy, placing neatly cut portions of potatoes and tomatoes into each large aquarium, all the while removing the no longer nutritious portions left over from yesterday. Ironically, they both wore the same clothes that they had on yesterday; Cockroach was now in his third straight day of wearing his.

Inside the big white house, Mother Maxine was busy once again at the stove preparing breakfast. The three kids sat the kitchen table hungry for a balanced meal. Whether the four of them knew about last night was unimportant. What was important to this family was making money, eating well, and knocking off all those who tried to disrupt the tradition of the Waller family. To the Waller family, their motto was plain and simple: only the strong survive in a world with economic crisis after crisis and a demanding need to take care of family first.

The Snowman

I have seen a lot of strange things in my days. But I tell you, nothing I've seen could be more horrible or in such a rage as to when the weather turns cold and it begins to snow. I've witnessed this strange event three times in the past forty years, or once every ten years, which means that my nerves are beginning to unravel because in another two months the snow will once again start falling out of the sky. And in Juneau, it snows a lot—to hell with that global warning crap!

The reason why I'm writing in this diary is because someone eventually has to know. An unknown force as this must be told eventually. No way will I live another hour of my life without jotting these words onto paper.

I was born and raised on the lower east side of Alaska in Juneau. I was the only child to two very strong and intellectual parents. They were proud to have me as their son. Even though they passed away when I was only sixteen, the lessons they instilled inside my brain was how to survive on my own with all this wildlife surrounding this beautiful state of Alaska, and those lessons have been a part of who I am all the way up to my current mature age of sixty-eight. The fact that I am physically fit, the same as my strong pop, was has aided in my wildlife survival.

You're probably wondering how they died. Well, while the three of us were strenuously trying to break a patch of ice on a subzero morning to catch fish for a healthy breakfast, neither one of us noticed the adult female polar bear camped out just ten yards from where we were fishing, perfectly blending into her surroundings, burying herself in around three feet of snow, camouflaged out of sight. As my father finally broke the ice and began to yank a three- to four-pound cod out of the icy waters— my father actually wanted to catch a halibut, a much bigger and better-flavored fish—out of the corner of our eyes the white earth just stood straight up, almost seeming to touch the sky. Within a couple of seconds, a huge white paw slashed deeply into my mom's and pop's faces simultaneously; I began to run immediately from witnessing all the warm red liquids splatter onto the rock-solid ice.

When I got home I immediately locked the front door and proceeded to also lock myself inside the bedroom closet. The positive influence that came from this negative situation was I learned quickly how to be a better fisherman in the winter, to always be cautious of my surroundings.

Now, what I've seen over the past years has nothing to do with my parents' death, or surviving on my own. What I want the world to know is that an evil lurks in these parts of the wilderness. There is no telling as to how long this evil has lived around here, or any other place where it snows. The sad part is that in this small section of town no one knows of this evil, or they don't bother to discuss this matter and feel that it's better to just keep silent. Maybe they are just too afraid to talk, or they are in disbelief. I am without a doubt all of the above.

The first incident happened when I was only twenty-eight years old, but I still remember the slashing of my folks as if it just happened yesterday. I was actually being inquisitive, watching a traveling man looking for a quiet place to rest from hunting some large game; his giant shotgun proved this point because there was actually no animal small enough to remain intact after hit by one of the gun's gigantic shells. I hadn't seen anyone for weeks, with the snow piling up and all. Then, all of a sudden, headlights caught my attention beaming through my kitchen window. The driver stopped in front of a vacant house just thirty yards from where I lived. Being vastly alert to any sign of movement, I watched the driver stop in front of the house, get out of his large pickup truck, and tread up to the house's front door; he almost slipped on the steps, which were recently covered by fluffy white powder. I was curious as to how his truck had no snow covering, even though it was covered in minutes as large snowflakes descended from the sky. I thought that maybe he had a garage at home or he knew someone close by who just happened to have a garage themselves. The wind was now picking up speed, the large snowflakes blowing in all sorts of directions.

Out of my peripheral vision I saw movement in the large humps of snow. I began to pray that a polar bear wouldn't attack the man, remembering the incident with my parents. I was breathing so hard, and it was so cold outside, I was forced to wipe the window with the sleeve of my right arm, concerned not to miss anything currently taking place.

Then, the snow just rose in an indignant manner. The snow formed as high as ten feet into the air. To my surprise, arms, legs, chest, and a large prodigious head formed within the snow. Next, a gaping mouth that was full of shark-like teeth became clearly visible even at this thirty-yard distance. But those two monstrous black eyes sent me into a state of delirium.

What I witnessed next was a torn and battered traveling man quickly engulfed at the mercy of the snow. The snow just horribly formed out of nowhere! *This can't be the information my eyes are directing to my brain! Was this actually what I just saw?* These thoughts raced through my mind at a thousand miles per hour. I immediately began to squint my eyes to make sure that my foggy window and the oncoming snow did not distort my vision. The final part of the traveling man's body to be devoured was his heart, which was still beating in the frigid air.

For the remainder of the winter season, I felt sick and appeared glum. I knew right then that this incident would be inside my mind for the rest of my life.

I've always enjoyed every year of my life. I am very thankful that my parents did not owe any money on the house after they died. This part of the country is mostly wilderness, so there's always plenty to eat. When you have no housing or food bills it's okay to live in a climate that's cool for half of the year and extremely cold the other half. I just have to chop up a tree every now and then to provide warmth and adequate light.

And when the snow gets so high that it overtakes the top of my house, instead of sitting around and getting bored, I just dig deep into the back of the utility closet in the basement and pull out a pair of snow skies to practice some short dives down a neighboring embankment; I start on the roof of the house.

Now, one day I was deep into the forest looking for game; mainly I had the taste for a fluffy white rabbit. During the hunt, my past came rushing back to haunt me. I had ventured deep into the woods unsuccessfully on my hunt. The snow was falling down so heavy you could actually *smell* it. The forest of thin and narrow-crowned shore pines were completely covered in snow. You had to narrow your eyes to look up at the sky, which was a spooky dark-gray color. My nose was so cold the moisture escaping through my nostrils froze solid onto my mustache. Every step I took my feet would disappear in the surrounding whiteness. I had my father's shotgun on my shoulder, waiting for some game to appear.

Up ahead about fifty yards I could barely make out someone who also seemed to be hunting, for what I didn't know. As a matter of fact, the hunter was pointing a rifle into the direction of something that had caught his attention.

Ka-boom!

The shot was deafening in the silent and frigid forest. But he didn't move at all after the shot. He just stood in his position like a statue for nearly thirty seconds.

Ka-boom!

A second shot. But instead of remaining like a statue, he began to walk into the direction where his rifle was aimed; it was as if he had hit his target.

Then, the unthinkable happened. As he slowly walked through the deep snow, struggling with each and every step to get closer to his target, behind him the snow magically rose high into the air. But in this incident, there was a slight difference in appearance from what I witnessed so horribly ten years ago. The snow seemed to be more massive, as if gaining weight. The snow creature was gaining weight after feeding all these years.

But just like ten years ago, I thought the being in front of me was just a hungry polar bear. My memory quickly reminded me that this was no animal, but some type of satanic monster, even though I could barely see with all the snow falling.

This aberrant behavior of what was not supposed to be happening enclosed me into a state of hysteria. I was on the verge of needing mouth-to-mouth resuscitation, but not from that monster in front of me.

The snow began to make some sort of low-pitched humming. This beast was becoming exuberant—as if it had feelings—as to what it was about to do to the hunter.

Ten years ago, I was in self-denial at what I saw; I was constantly trying to trick my brain into a thinking, *This is not real*. But watching the hunter's body being ripped apart as if ten large butcher knives were at work was about as real as this horror could get.

This time, the deep snow did nothing to slow my progress as I began to run as fast as I could. I didn't turn around to see if this monstrous beast was chasing after me, but I could feel those large dark eyes on the back of my neck all the way home, goose bumps aiding in the increased speed of my heart.

Once I arrived home, I quickly found some unused plywood in the garage and boarded up as many windows as

I could, including those in the garage. I was too afraid that just in case I was actually being followed, I wanted to play it on the safe side as much as possible. I was slamming down so hard on the hammer the palm on my right hand was a dark pink. For a while I had difficulty with self-control.

As the years fly by, your mind will eventually begin to forget certain things, especially if it's been more than a few years. The mind can only retain but so much, no matter how wonderful or tragic the events are. But what my mind tried to erase was coming back again. I was now ready to declare under oath that this monstrous thing performs its satanic evil once every ten years. Either that, or it kills in my neck of the woods every ten years; surely someone else alive now must have been face-to-face with this evil being.

Now, for the third time that I have seen this monster, it has appeared at a different time. Since the two previous times I have seen the beast, my watches informed me it was around early evening, just before night, except when the nights last for thirty days straight, which forced me to stock up my freezer. I did remember that I decided to change my hunting patterns over the years by going out in the early morning hours, terrified to ever see this snowy monster ever again. I arose around six in the morning, sniffing the shirt that was hanging on my closet door from the previous day to see if the cotton was still fresh. After the fresh-test approval, I began to get dressed. Just when

I was stuffing my right arm through the shirt, my ears picked up a soft *whooshing* sound outside my window. I figured that it was just a bald eagle gathering some small prey. But after I finished putting the shirt on, I heard that same *whooshing* sound again. Strange though, the sound was beginning to lull me into a state of peace and happiness, even though the sound would eventually turn out to be the evilest noise that I would ever hear for as long as I live, something I would find out later on in life.

I walked to the front door and opened it. The subzero temperature smacked me right in the face, awakening me from a tired it-would-be-nice-to-stay-in-bed mentality; the wind chill made it seem as though the sun was unable to produce any heat at all. Even though the door was half opened, I could clearly see what was making the soft *whooshing* sound. Small patches of snow were lined up in perfect formation, magically bunny-hopping on cue as if being ordered by some unknown superior power.

I jumped back into the living room and carefully closed the front door, fighting off all the fear I had inside to not allow a loud scream to burst through my lungs. As I held back the scream, all of my inward organs tightened up. I also did not demur to what I had just witnessed.

I rushed to the window to see exactly what was going on, especially since it was not snowing and the sun shone brightly over the new patches of snow. What I saw were lumps of snow—about ten of them, I think—forming together in two different directions. They were heading toward a large dead carcass just outside my window. It was as if the snow could smell blood. I could identify the dead carcass, which was a deer. I had no idea as to how the large animal died because I didn't notice any wounds on the body parts that I could see, or a sign of injury; also, I could not see any drops of blood. But what was strange about the dead animal's appearance was the way it lay on its back with all four legs pointing straight up toward the clear blue sky, frozen solid as a rock in death. The animal's tongue hung out the left side of its mouth as if jokingly laughing at the oncoming snow. The dead carcass looked to be ready to be placed into a sarcophagus.

The snow lumps quickly gathered around the stiff carcass and strangely paused for a moment. Then, the white lumps gathered over top the deer, completely covering the fresh death, writhing and squirming at the dead carcass, resembling a white miniature mountain with movement.

About an hour later, the lumps of snow began to descend backward. The pink piles of snow were haughty after the feeding, leaving only the animal's skeleton, and the legs were still pointing toward the sky.

After another ten minutes passed, the lumps of snow gathered into one heap. As the pinkish beast stood straight up, it looked more frightening than ever before. How those clawed fingers and dark black eyes popped into place out of nowhere, I have the slightest clue.

Another ten years have passed since I've seen this evil that I just recently labeled, very intelligently I might add, The Snowman. I know the name sounds more like a name for a character during the holidays, but what other name would be more appropriate? That's what I saw three times in my life: a destructive force coming right out of something as soft and fluffy as snow.

I had nightmares before, but now I have illusions in the day *and* night. My mind will never forget this evil like I forgot a few other things that happened earlier in my life. This is why I need to let someone else know; spreading this news may ease my conscious a little. I didn't want to notify the town's newspaper because even though we all need to read the papers to keep up with what's going on in the world, sometimes the papers keep us misinformed with twisted tales that don't educate us at all. But no matter what, this story will probably still make the local newspaper, and many will not believe a single word of it; hell, the newspaper's editor probably won't believe it either.

So, when the mailman comes later on, I am going to give him this letter to deliver to the governor of Alaska. One, I hope they don't think I'm insane. And two, I pray that someone will definitely believe my words. Why? Because I'm too old to do anything constructive to destroy this beast, and this beast will be ready to make another evil appearance in this part of the earth in only a short period of time.

The Latest Attraction

Z ane Hook sat in the living room quarters of his mobile trailer staring into space, listening to the silence outside, a silence that was supposed to be filled with laughter, screams, and music. The silence was deafening as it swarmed all around him and throughout the dwelling, causing him to almost go insane. He couldn't believe that once again a new city would not have gaiety—even though it was opening night and the weather was perfectly mild—toward his carnival.

He jumped when he heard himself snore as he dozed off to sleep. This was the only excitement of the day, adding to his disappointment.

When he looked out the window at the skyline of carnival rides and didn't see any patrons, he almost cried. A thought raced through his mind of going out and turning on all of the rides just to make certain they still operated properly. Overhead, exactly between the rows of rides, a crescent-shaped moon seemed to be smiling at him, as if in humiliation.

Zane knew that life had endless opportunities if you wanted to become successful. He figured that he could always open a new exhibit to show off his well-maintained body; despite the fact that he was not very muscular, women still adored his body. At thirty-eight and still good-looking, tall, and athletic, maybe the new attraction could be whatever woman could luckily guess his age, the prize would be to offer her a date. But he quickly shook off the idea, knowing that his employees might think of him as a dolt.

The tension of losing money created more perspiration on his face than the early summer heat. The sweat was good for him since a stream of the perspiration trickled into the corner of his left eye, breaking his concentration from the negative atmosphere of the carnival. If some great idea was not thought of soon to bring patrons into the carnival in swarms, this show would be in financial ruins. Something needed to be done soon, as in yesterday, to get not just this town, but the following cities on the tour, to make the event better than your average small-town county fair.

Actually, the carnival was not too bad. It was just not great. A Ferris wheel and merry-go-round were the star attractions. A spider ride and a haunted house that had real actors and actresses instead of mechanics anchored the first two rows to be at least a satisfactory form of entertainment; the haunted house was okay but not too frightening. But his live shows—belly dancers, a man changing into a gorilla, a horse the size of a penis—actually sucked. A deformed-looking monkey and a large lady claiming to have the biggest tits on earth were okay if you were easily befogged, but not enough to spread the word across town. What the carnival needed was a bizarre-looking attraction, the way carnivals operated in the good old days, and Zane knew this. He slammed his fist on the right arm of the sofa defiantly, knowing that all the resources he had left would probably be drained well before next year's season, which was only nine months away.

Before settling his body down to prepare for bed, he drew out plans on a new attraction that just might get him through the end of this season. Part of the plan included a young ape he unbelievably stole from the North Carolina Zoo in Asheboro a couple of years ago. News reports of an ape being stolen from any zoo blended in perfectly with the chaos of idiot behavior that regularly makes the morning and evening news, so it was perfect that the story died out as fast as it was reported, partly because it was so unbelievable. The ape was becoming too large to financially take care of and too large to hide in the back of the trailer unnoticeably. Also, the ape was now big and strong enough to burst through the cage that was initially designed to keep him in when he was first kidnapped. To make a long story short, it was time to start making something in return. The attraction would be titled: Bruno: The Great Ape!

Much later that night, Zane tossed and turned as he dreamed. His girlfriend, Summer Ray, was standing over him as he lay on his back in bed. She had tied his four limbs to the four corners of the bed. She was mysteriously nine months pregnant and about to deliver, even though she laughed incessantly and also fondled her breasts. Then she lay on her back beside him, spread her legs as far apart as she could, and out came a hairy infant that made all sorts of screaming noises as the little creature struggled out of her vagina. This was a spine-chilling event for Zane, a horrendous script placed into his adventurous mind, when the hairy-looking creature gained the strength to move on its own and began to chew on his limbs tied to the bedposts.

He woke up and immediately ran outside from the trailer into the darkness. The damp perspiration on his clothing and the chill of the late night collided to wake him up, but not before he stumbled over a stack of ropes and cables connected between a large generator and the haunted house.

When he turned around, Bruno was standing in the front door of the trailer. The ape looked concerned for his master of the past two years, and Zane immediately recognized the look on the beast's face. Normally when an ape breaks loose, the animal would pummel the first living being in its sight, and Zane knew this after years of studying the giant monkeys. He also knew that the animal had to appreciate how it was fed and generously treated, and probably looked at his master as a parent rather than any other human since Zane snatched the ape at such a young age.

A sick idea raced through Zane's mind.

Bruno grunted and treaded two steps inside the trailer.

The beast reminded Zane of the recent dream.

Bruno treaded two more steps forward, grunting and squealing.

Not only could Bruno be an attraction, Zane thought....

The ape was now standing over his master.

Zane would not need a ghostwriter for this carnival script. This script will be from his own thoughts and imagination.

Summer Ray Midland and Zane were now in their eighth year of dating. Even though he never asked her to jump the broom—something her family currently disapproved—she still felt the same love for him as she did when they first started dating. But it was pure luck for him to find a girl who had two previous devastating relationships prior to this current one. And Zane knew that it wouldn't take much to please her, even though he loved going the extra mile in affection for her every once in a while.

They first met on a blind date at a carnival, where he juggled operating various rides and games. She thought that dating someone in this type of environment was very interesting, considering the fact that her last two lovers were then, and still are now, in the banking industry. She felt that Zane's occupation was the description of someone who was not looking for so much in a woman, as her other boyfriends brought home almost every weekday evening the pressures of dealing with the struggling financial industry in America.

What she loved most about him was the way he always complimented her figure, his willingness to help in the kitchen, how he occasionally did both of their laundry, and how she could easily fit into some of his clothes, especially his sleepwear. To sum up what she loved about him: he was to her the ideal man who every woman could easily fall in love with.

She felt that he would be her lover forever. She would do anything for him. And when he suggested to her about taking the sperm three months ago from Bruno, and how her commitment could improve the carnival's future, she took no resistance while sprawling onto the bed to receive the ape's sperm, which was securely kept in a sealed sandwich bag and placed in the refrigerator for preservation. All she wanted was for no one in the world—especially her demanding family—to know that she would become pregnant from the privacy of the non-human beast.

Zane actually fed her mind with a bunch of bull about how man originally came into existence from a slumped over ape in the first place, only learning to stand up straight after thousands of years of evolution. But like most humans, she never thought about the fact that if man was originally an ape, where did all the black hairs covering the body disappear to?

If only she knew that no matter how much love someone has for another, the act was still insane, but not as insane as the act her boyfriend performed by masturbating the ape. Maybe this was why they were still together, because opposites attract, but deep down inside, to fall in love means you have to have *something* in common.

Five years have gone by since the child's birth. Summer Ray could not believe that she was not adamant when Zane approached her about taking the sperm. It was just hard for her to defend his cogent attitude toward the subject, knowing that he was the bread winner, and she did feel as if the idea could make lots of money.

She was exactly right. The carnival still boasted the same rides, attractions, and games. Every city they went to Zane and his crew would line every ride, game, and show in the same exact position, creating the same shadows on the ground, making them both feel somewhat at home while on the road. But two new attractions boosted the carnival's finances to a sum large enough to keep the carnival going and making all the employees happy: Bruno, The Great Ape, which was second on the ticket list, but was far behind the number one attraction, Lucifer's Golden Child. Summer Ray didn't even want to know where or how her boyfriend brought this ugly thing into his business, except for the fact that she was still right that her child's birth would also be a financial stabilizer, even though every time her family asked when she and Zane planned on having children, she would almost throw up right in front of them.

Over the past few years, Zane and Summer Ray never mentioned anything about Bruno to one another. They both acted as if the child just popped out of the thin air, walking past one another while barely speaking, and the fact that Zane was too busy calculating bags full of cash after each and every stop they made while on tour was actually the main reason why nothing was said.

Summer Ray made the decision to sneak to the doctor to get fixed so that she couldn't have any more children; Zane silently backed her 100 percent. She just couldn't see anything else coming out of her vagina, even if the child *was* normal, because she knew that she would be too ashamed to say who their half brother was, since Zane was not the father. The fright that shocked her the most was when she couldn't decide at her first birth to make out of the bloody mess of what to keep and what to throw away.

Every night as they lay in bed she would always position herself to look out the trailer's bedroom window toward the attraction with the big yellow board with a baby that resembled something as ugly as any being could ever be painted, and the other red sign adjacent to it that showed her child. Even though the creature she birthed was no longer a baby, she insisted on the painting staying the same exact way as originally drawn. When she could finally manage to fall asleep, the same nightmare of her having an ape-like baby would wake her screaming in a fit with sweat all over her body. She began to pray every day and night that the dreams wouldn't last for the rest of her life.

Strangely to her, the man who lay beside her and comforted her to go back to sleep had this same nightmare over five years ago.

Sand Boy

Born on a farm and accustomed to playing in the dirt, Ian Dowser loved to draw figures on the earth whenever he could find a handful of loose soil. Now still young, his parents regularly fussed at him for always getting his body and clothes into a filthy mess. He stayed dirty so much the kids at school didn't call him by the name his parents assigned to him, but instead joked out loud that his name should have been Sand Boy at birth.

But that didn't stop his parents from purchasing a larger stake of land in a rural part of North Carolina. And they joyfully purchased the land because it was so cheap; nearly half of the one hundred acres was mainly dust, and the fine worthless particles would blow into your eyes with just the slightest breeze.

Ian was now nine and getting dirtier than ever before. He found so much time to go out and play while unattended by his father, who was always expressing uncritical praise and affection to his lovely wife, Valentine; she was always blushing, her face aching at the cheeks regularly. His only wish was not for his parents to stop loving and caring for one another, but for them to have an avenue for their only child to walk through to get some much-needed attention at home. If so, maybe he wouldn't have to spend so much time playing out in the sand in the first place.

On this unusual hot and sticky day, Ian decided to go deeper into the farm's dry acres, knowing that he would have the privilege to draw as much as he wanted. The heavy rains had come earlier in the evening and cooled off the parched earth. The dust had settled for now into small lukewarm clumps but was still manageable to work with for the miniature artist. But today would be *very* unusual for Ian, not because the rain may cause some difficulty in his earthly creation by settling most of the dust, and not just because it was Samhain.

His pace stopped at the site of an old wooden house, which was beaten badly by the constantly changing weather and lack of upkeep over the years. Most of the shingles were partially gone, and the shutters were either missing or suspended from their original foundation. The house resembled a large hovel that was used in the past as a lair. No vegetation was able to survive on this dry area of the farm.

Ian stared at the ugly house in front of him.

He quickly remembered how his parents would always preach about how you can judge a person by their appearance and the condition of their house. He thought, *Whoever used to live here, or currently lives here, is as filthy as I will ever be.*

Somehow, his mind snapped into a trance. As the wind began to stir, the shutters and shingles attached to the ugly house began to wince in pain; the lad felt that the house must be bleeding inside from all this pain.

He snapped right out of his trance and remembered why he came out here in the first place: to play in the sand. From the evening heat, the dirt quickly became so loose he easily grabbed two large handfuls of the worthless earth. Just like always, the images recorded in the back of his mind would form gracefully onto the earth as the grains of sand freely released from his hands.

The shingles and shudders moaned again in the breeze.

Ian continued to draw until a dragon appeared in front of his feet, a dragon he remembered from watching an afternoon cartoon yesterday while relaxing from a busy day at school. The dragon appeared as a clearly drawn image, almost exactly the way the original cartoonist drew it on the television show. Anyone who happened to stumble onto one of his creations would quickly think that a mature, seasoned artist was at work, despite his young age.

This time, the shingles and shudders sounded as if

they were going to explode off their hinges, but the wind had unnoticeably stopped blowing.

Ian was now curious about the house, why now the dwelling was creating so much noise in the quiet surroundings. With each step he took toward the house, his feet somehow glided in the loose sand, but not enough for him to lose his balance.

He peeped into one of the windows through a set of dusty glass panes. He thought he noticed movement but considered the dusty panes were just playing tricks on his mind.

Behind him, the sand began to stir.

Ian surveyed the entire room through the dusty panes, not wanting to actually see anything, but just making sure. If the panes were clear of their filth, he would have seen one of the strangest of all women ever created on earth float in thin air up the house's rotted stairs, but to his advantage his vision was blocked. He was surprised at how chilly the surroundings of the house were.

The sand continued to stir on the semi-dry earth, but no sound emerged.

Ian saw movement again. Only he didn't know, through the dusty panes, that the movement was behind him, not in front of him in the large living room.

The dragon stood at least eight feet tall, its grayish-beige color blending in almost unseen against the overcast sky.

Once the house was uninteresting to Ian, he turned to put the finishing touches onto his artwork. When he saw the creature towering high into the air, he realized what the definition of being stuck between a rock and a hard place was: in front of him was this magical creature from out of nowhere; behind him was this huge spooky-looking house.

As he ran, this time he almost slipped on the loose earth, but fear aided him in keeping his balance. The fear did not just come from his surroundings, but when he realized that his house was so far away, the thought of being devoured alive was just not on the agenda for today.

When he managed to reach a large patch of grass he totally regained his footing, picking up much-needed speed. Now, nothing would be able to stop him from reaching home safely, the same way a base runner feels after leaving third and making it to home plate on a sacrifice fly to the outfield. Tears began to trickle down his soft cheeks from the sight of the monstrosity just seconds ago in front of him.

He was shocked when he glanced behind himself and the dragon was not on his heels. He had no idea where the large piles of skeletons surrounding the house came from; there were so many bones he could make them out even though he was many yards from where he stood earlier. Now he was able to slow his pace down enough to catch his breath. He vowed at that moment to never play in the sand again.

Now inside his house, he glanced through his bedroom window, peeping behind the curtains, terrified to see the monstrous creature again. The fact that he knew this creature was created from his artwork sent shivers up and down his spine.

There it was. The creature could be seen in the distance from the house standing at the edge of where grass met the sand. Ian realized then that what he drew must not be able to maneuver on the grass; he was very thankful for this.

Inside his bedroom he felt safe, the way a child always feels safe after facing danger and then later being in the comfort of his parents' surroundings. He could hear them in the hallway whispering to one another, but suddenly this didn't bother him at all.

But the safety of his parents didn't do him any good when suppertime came. All of a sudden, he was afraid to eat one of his mom's favorite dishes—black-eyed peas. After the terror he saw just a few hours ago, somehow he became afraid to eat the black-eyed peas because he thought the eyes of the peas would be looking around inside his stomach as soon as they descended down his throat, even though he never felt this way about eating one of his favorite dishes before this evening. He didn't realize that all he had to do was what his mother had always reminded him to do while eating in the past: "Just chew your food very good, son, and anything you eat will digest properly."

Over the next few days, Ian was ashamed to tell anyone of what he created and later saw form out of the sand. He knew the only responses thrown at him would be that kids just have the wildest of imaginations.

Much of the sandy surface was visible on his way to school. The dragon he drew always met him at the edge of grass near a man-made path; the creature could maneuver anywhere on the sand as freely as the sand could blow in the wind. Though terrified, he still took the same route. He thought that disguising himself to look like some other kid would deter the dragon from noticing him, but it was as if the dragon knew his scent because he only appeared while Ian was either walking to school, coming home from school, or even just traveling by with his parents in the family car.

For this young boy, reality met head-on with the essence of magic. For it was on this farm that his parents bought for a very cheap price, in front of that ugly house he saw shortly after the property was purchased, that nearly one hundred years ago a large group of witches, who had a coven to practice witchcraft, were brutally executed to death by local townspeople who made a solemn promise to rid the land of those who put the devil's work before God's religion. If only he knew about the execution of the witches, he could probably figure out that's where the numerous piles of skeletons came from.

Ian will always remember his work, particularly the bad happenings at the house, but also the good things of which included the fact that as a young boy he was already so creative in the field of art.

Now some years later, he teaches the craft of drawing, rather than drawing himself, still not able to reconcile that his last drawing only appeared to him as if straight out of hell because of where this drawing took place, not because his work was evil.

Death to Halloween

The Bible study lasted for nearly two hours, but no one was bored. It was one of the best sermons Reverend John Williams had ever preached; he actually was supposed to be teaching. Well, he always preached his best sermons when the calendar showed Halloween was right around the corner.

Reverend Williams preached so dramatically around this time of the year because all he wanted was to be forgiven for the horrible acts he performed in childhood on Halloween nights from the past. And even though it was Tuesday and not the regular Wednesday-night study session, that didn't do anything to stop him from gathering his congregation on this day at noon; surprisingly, lots of worshippers showed up. Throughout the year, he was comfortable with the trials, tribulations, and joy that came every day he woke up above ground, but turning to the ministry ten years ago still did not block his past from memory.

After the sermon, he did his normal after service routine: greeting the congregation as they escaped past him through the church doors, followed by wishing them a blessed and prosperous week ahead. He always stood to the left of the exit doors as the congregation walked out, making it easier to hold out his right hand—the hand that was used for so many juvenile devilish acts—for greeting the worshippers.

On this particular day in 2023, things drastically changed for Reverend John Williams. As he drove down Water Street—always taking the same route home after service—all his past Halloween pranks and jokes came back to haunt him in a way he never imagined. He quickly considered the year thirteen to be an unlucky one to start any type of profession but decided quickly that ministers ought not to think in such a suspicious way. In addition, he knew plenty of folks who had birthdays on the thirteenth, athletes who wore number thirteen, wedding anniversaries celebrating thirteen years of marriage, and so on.

After driving a few blocks, he noticed that he wasn't on Water Street anymore. Instead, he found himself on State Street, the neighborhood he grew up in as a teenager in 1961. But this also took him off his route, as the car seemed to be driving on its own powers. When he looked out the driver's side window he saw a young boy—identical to himself as a youngster—trashing Ruth Akers's house with roll after roll of toilet tissue. John knew even as a youngster that Ruth was barely able to live on her own, because his own mother was one of the many caretakers who was pleased to assist her at any cost no matter what time of the day or night it was. He knew the youngster was him, even though daytime had changed quickly to dark, as he recognized the red-and-blue striped shirt and the blue jeans with holes in the knees that the kids in the neighborhood used to constantly pick on him regularly about. The bad impression on his younger self's face was enough to make the older version of himself burst out in tears as he sat behind the wheel of his car. His car stilled, as if he were watching a movie of himself at a drive-in theatre. When Ruth Akers stormed outside of her home yelling at a young John Williams, the reverend closed his eyes, knowing what was about to happen next; the old lady slipped on her steps and fell hard onto the concrete sidewalk, easily snapping her neck in half. The case is still unsolved after all these years.

John could not figure out why he was viewing this all of a sudden, just after church service. His hands began to shake on the steering wheel, as he was unable to make out any images through the rearview mirror.

Now the car began to slowly move again. The time of day again moved parallel with the car, to the exact time he yet again performed another act of grief to someone else. After a short drive, he ended up on Adams Street. When the car stopped, the reverend was in front of Boo Green's Corner Mart. John saw another younger version of himself again, this time in 1963. The young boy walked from behind the store up to the entrance. He clearly remembered that this was when he bought a pack of razor blades, inserting one into an apple that was later bitten by a mentally ill young girl named Claudia Whitman, destroying her family's ambitions of ever celebrating Halloween ever again. Before the ambulance arrived, Claudia had bled to death from a deep gash wound into her lower left jaw.

Reverend John Williams was still unable to see anything through his rearview mirror except for his childhood acts. He turned quickly to look out the car's back window, to see if this was some sort of crazy illusion; his old neck popped loudly from the quick turn. There was nothing in view from behind except total darkness, as if looking into the pits of hell, because the sun still shone brightly overhead.

The car started moving again magically, because his foot was not pressing down on the gas pedal, and neither of his arms was on the steering wheel. When he looked down between his legs and noticed that his right foot was not pressing the gas pedal, he immediately started begging God to forgive him of all his sins, even more than when earlier in life he pleaded with Christ to come and save his evil soul as if his spirit knew what was about to happen one day sooner or later. Only he didn't realize deep down inside that God had already forgiven him, but he had not forgiven himself, keeping these thoughts of his past locked deep inside the back of his mind. If only he would've confessed these sins years ago this day, or night, they probably would never have even taken place.

Day immediately changed back to night. John saw himself as a youngster for the third time, in 1964, standing outside a fence on Andrews Avenue. Inside the fence was three large Dobermans, one red and two black. The dogs belonged to Bubba Foster, known throughout the neighborhood as "Pops" because he always had positive information to explain to kids who seemed to be going in the wrong direction and heading into a life of living behind bars: those involved with drugs, robbery, and other petty crimes. In young John's right hand he held a yellow box of rat poison that he swiped from underneath the bathroom sink at home.

His younger self snuck food from the evening's supper and laced things with a heap of the poison. He giggled as he threw food over the fence, which quickly quieted the barking dogs. A few moments later, the rat poison sent the dogs into a total frenzy, snarling with their teeth and foaming at the mouth.

Bubba arrived home a short time after a young John Williams finished yet a third act of grief to someone. And when Bubba opened up the gates—which will immediately become the Gates of Sheol—the vicious Dobermans tore his strong black body to pieces. After the attack, Bubba looked like a perfect Halloween yard decoration along with a stream of blood for special effects as he lay lifeless on the grass. As a matter of fact, those who walked by didn't even see anything wrong with the decoration, even the way the dogs looked while dying and standing still with their now white-covered faces; a few even complimented Bubba's hard work.

John just stood still behind a row of bushes, still giggling as if this were the funniest thing he had ever witnessed in his young life.

Behind the wheel of the car, the current version of John Williams was so soaked his suit stuck to his body.

Suddenly, the reverend was back in 2023. His heart raced rapidly in his chest as he sat behind the wheel. His face was now hot as if the cool temperature outside had turned to a mid-summer hot day. Between his legs, moisture developed into a round circle, darkening his gray suit just a bit more.

On Halloween night, John sat by the living-room window watching kids trick-or-treat up and down the neighborhood sidewalks. No one came to his door because the front porch light was off.

The reflections of three individuals appeared in the window as he looked out, letting the reverend know that three individuals were behind him. As he turned around, he saw Ruth, Claudia, and Bubba, over sixty years since their deaths. He was in awe at how they looked the same as they did at the time of their deaths, only they didn't smell too bad. The scene reminded him that his past was not completely forgotten.

He rushed into his bedroom and opened the closet door, fumbling frantically under a pile of clothes. Under the pile of clean clothes that were just recently washed he found what he was looking for as his hand went cold by gripping the steel object. After being saved, he refused to give up the .44 Magnum that belonged to his late father. Now, this same gun fired and blew his brains back into the closet, exactly where the gun was being hid for so many years; he died so quickly he didn't even hear the loud laughter coming from the living-room.

After his death, everyone who knew him was per-plexed at how he died on Halloween night, the same way the ones who knew his three victims didn't understand the way they died on Halloween night many years ago as well.

Keep Out

The walk was long, and they needed the rest. They did not plan on being in the woods this long. They needed a break from the August heat and desperately needed to find a spot to cool off.

After walking for another ten minutes, they found that spot. An old shack was sitting peacefully under a few large eastern cottonwood trees where a few were tall enough to be seen almost at a mile distance, the old structure almost unseen until you were close to it. The paint on the shack had worn completely off over time; now the old building looked dingy gray. The wood holding the shack together had cracks in nearly all the planks. A rusted white sign with red letters inside of it read: ASHCROFT SLAUGHTERHOUSE—ESTABLISHED 1949.

Michael found out that the door at the front of the shack had settled over time, as it cried in a high pitch when he grabbed, turned, and pulled the knob, having to force it open. Spider webs were everywhere. Eight-legged creatures rushed from the daylight and ran abroad toward any dark area they could find. Michael jumped back from the sight as if he had arachnophobia. Dust weightlessly flowed through the cracks from the inside. The only thing that didn't move was the insects that were caught in the spiders' webs; they were helplessly suspended in midair.

Danny proudly shouted out loud, "I'm not going in there!"

When Michael got the nerve to briefly glance through the opening, he realized that a fallen branch that his left foot was stepping on could be used to knock some of the cobwebs down to make the inside a little safer. He was scared, but not as afraid as Danny.

After clearing the entrance, Michael, now bold, looked at his friends and asked, "Why are you guys so afraid of everything? We have a long way to go, and all four of us need a rest and a break from all this summer heat."

And Michael was right. All four of the boys were sweating so hard that they looked as if they had just stepped out of a swimming pool; their foreheads were steadily dripping sweat and showed an outline on each one's chest. Dehydration would soon be in the picture if the boys didn't find relief soon.

Inside, three of them rushed to a bench that was set up adjacent to one of the walls. Michael was first to take off his shirt and somehow tried to wipe the sweat from his face. Steven and Danny did the same as well. Ten minutes later, the three of them were all enjoying the break from the hot late-summer sun.

Terrance was still standing outside in the heat; it seems that Danny was not the most frightened one after all. "I'm not a big fan of old slaughterhouses. I'm also not a big fan of creepy bugs, especially black widow spiders. That red spot on their backside gives me the creeps." After quivering he added, "Those things can kill a human, you know." But after being convinced by Michael—who jokingly said that it was so hot, the authorities would later find him fried like an egg on the ground—of how cool it was inside, he joined the crew on the wooden bench.

"I overheard my grandfather telling one of his buddies about a slaughterhouse in these parts of the woods." Steven was not much of the talkative type, but he felt he had to tell this particular story.

"Oh, yeah?" Terrance wanted to know more. "Like what?"

"Well," Steven continued, "he was telling the man who owns the peach farm up the road, Mr. Henry, that a family had a successful business slaughtering hogs and goats, taking the meat and selling it to nearby neighborhood farm stores. But one day one of the brothers, who owned a big part of the business, went psycho and killed his entire family. All of them! Including cousins, aunts, uncles... Well, you get the picture."

The other three stared in awe at Steven as he told the horror story.

"Why did he do that?" Terrance asked.

"Well, the way my grandfather was explaining the story to Mr. Henry was that he accused his family of not giving him his fair share of the profits. So, one day he came home tired, upset, and angry. He had been going around to the farm stores all day and got an estimate of how much meat his family had actually been selling, just out of curiosity."

"But couldn't he have worked out something with his family?" Danny asked.

"Probably not," Steven replied. "You see, my grandfather said the man was slow with learning and was left back a grade in school at least three times because he wasn't smart enough to pass his classes. Everyone in school would pick on him for being slow, even his own brothers. His family apparently thought he was stupid because they all had degrees, and he just had a fourth-grade education. But the fact that he couldn't pass history or English and get a high school diploma didn't mean he was slow at counting money."

"What was his name?" Michael asked.

"I think it was Bryan Ashcroft, but I can't remember exactly."

The four boys sat silent for a moment, no sweat pouring, enjoying the break from the sun. The coolness inside sort of eased the fear of the horror story.

Two black widow spiders crawled on the ceiling, probably still looking for dark shelter.

Outside, a bird landed on the front entrance of the shack where the boys had just recently entered. All four of them looked in that direction. The bird's shadow could be seen on the wall through a hole in the ceiling. The bird flew off quickly, as if being disturbed by something.

A few minutes later, finally being cooled off, the four boys agreed that they could possibly make it the rest of the way home. And as soon as they all stood up, they could hear the branches on some of the large trees being swayed back and forth.

When Michael took one step toward the front door, one of the holes in the walls was quickly covered up from the outside. Even though sunlight was creeping through cracks throughout the shack, that one hole sent a chill through the boys as if the entire place had become completely dark.

Terrance was dripping water again—but not from sweat—as he felt the grayish pupil eye socket was looking directly at him. He was staring so hard that he could also make out blood vessels in the eye where the color was supposed to be white.

Danny was about to release some bodily fluids himself but changed his mind as the eye left the hole and sunlight once again shone through.

Steven stood closest to where the boys had earlier sat on the bench. He felt safer being as far away from the eye as possible. Well, at least until behind him came an ax that cut through the wall so ferociously that wood went flying everywhere; the bench was cut in half.

Sunlight poured through the shack.

The black widows once again went scrambling for darkness.

All four of the boys rushed for the entrance door; the door was stuck. The human-like thing that made the hole in the wall was now waving his arm through the gigantic hole he created, almost grabbing Steven. The hand looked like dead flesh with the skin flaking off, and the sleeve of the blue-checked shirt the thing was wearing was so dirty it was hard to make out where the cuffs were from the skin.

With the boys trying to push the entrance door open, and that thing trying to get in, the shack swayed a little. As it did so, hundreds of black widow spiders descended from the ceiling and landed all over the boys and the thing's arms. The young men yelled and screamed, agitatedly trying to get the door open. The spiders were scrambling in all directions, as frightened as the boys. The thing didn't even notice the eight-legged creatures all over its arm.

The door finally opened. Before Michael, who was in front, could put one foot out the door, he slammed it back shut. Seeing a pig with half a head and blood dripping down the animal's right side was just too much for him to see.

The pig became a major distraction because as soon as the door was shut, a tall shadow crept inside the shack. When Steven turned around, he yelled as the thing stood right behind him with the ax raised high into the air, ready to slam down on the young boy's head.

The boys quickly formed a circle to defend themselves as one.

The ax whistled in the cool air of the shack and came down on Danny's neck so fast that the young boy's head hit the floor a second before the body had a chance to start tumbling down, eventually descending to the shack's floor like a cut tree.

Michael looked at his naked chest as the blood of Danny splashed everywhere. When Michael looked back up, the ax the thing was carrying hit him directly in the center of the forehead.

Terrance would be an easy third target because he began to vomit an orange-pink mass at the sight of seeing Michael's brains vibrate up and down, as if trying to find its protective skull.

Steven's quick thinking led him past the thing with the ax; the thing was focused squarely on Terrance. He almost slipped on an old sign that was lying face down on the ground; his friction caused the sign to turn over, having the words KEEP OUT, also written in red across a white background. As Steven ran through the forest, he could hear the volume of the screams of Terrance quieting the farther he got away from the shack. As he ran to safety, he couldn't even feel the briars and branches cutting away at his arms and legs, or feel the heat from the sun, as he was only focused on getting home.

Twenty minutes later, Steven was in the living-room of his home, scared to death, and bleeding down his arms and legs. When he stopped shaking and bleeding, he began to verify with his grandfather the story that was told about the slaughterhouse the Ashcroft family used to own and operate.

Daytime Vampires

By the time Scott and Hazel Howe made it to Henderson, North Carolina, it was already noon. The four-hour ride had been exhausting, mainly because they had to stop the damaged Honda Accord several times alongside the road to fix an assortment of problems, not surprising to them both since the used car salesman practically gave the car to them for free. The first week of September was already a warm and humid late morning ninety degrees, but not as hot as the weather was where they were driving from in Columbia, South Carolina. The humidity was generated mostly by the giant Kerr Lake, which stretched deeply into the southern parts of central Virginia and the northern parts of central North Carolina. The sky was only partly cloudy, barely giving relief from the heat every few minutes.

The couple was making the trip to Henderson to see the Vance Regional Botanical Garden, and to do some bass fishing in Kerr Lake, where it was said that the fish could grow to be as heavy as twenty-plus pounds. These two attractions were gaining lots of attention throughout the South the past few years and were now considered state tourist attractions. Both attractions were some of the biggest in their respectful categories in the entire country, bringing in thousands of dollars annually into the local economy, easing the pressures of tax revenue most small towns suffer deeply from; well at least that's what the advertisements explained.

"Well, we've finally made it," Scott said joyfully to his wife of seven wonderful and joyous years. But he was still not willing to throw the map into the glove-compartment just yet.

"Thank you, God!" she responded, trying to sound cheerful despite being a bit tired from the long and boring scenic drive up Highway 85 north. "Let's hurry inside and grab a couple of sodas," she demanded as Scott pulled into a BP gas station just off Exit 212 leading into Henderson.

"But we both agreed that water was the best solution in the daytime when it's hot and muggy outside. Remember?"

"Okay, enough with it," she agreed with a worn and ragged smile. "Let's just go inside and grab a couple of bottled waters for now and a couple of sodas for later on. How does that sound, honey?"

"That sounds just fine. You go get those valuable liquids for the body's stomach, and I'll pump some valuable liquid for the car's tank." He continued on a more serious note by adding, "We may be facing another problem with this lemon. Remember that I just gassed up in Charlotte, but the needle is already hugging E."

The Howe's were taking this trip to Henderson to do something different for the Labor Day holiday. Theme parks, museums, trips to major cities, and family reunions were making them both uninterested to celebrate. They could have visited the botanical garden back home, but this particular one had added attractions: a bat cave was adjacent to the garden; also, Scott had just recently earned his bachelor's degree in botany from the University of South Carolina, and he was already fascinated by seeing on the web how many different types of creatures the garden attracted every spring and summer; his wife thought it strange that he used the web for everything except directions.

Scott got back into the car after filling the lemon up to the rim and looked back at the map lying on the passenger's seat. He was excited to know that the garden and the lake were only six exits away. Before Hazel returned with the cold drinks, he managed to get a look through all the car windows at the surroundings. With Henderson being a small town, he was spooked at how much the city looked like some far-off land unusual to the look and feel of most American cities, especially after seeing a worn-down cemetery just across the street from the gas station, a building in need of renovation, and people who resembled creatures in a wax museum. Except these people were actually *real*.

But first things first. Before locating where they would be staying—the hotel was at a very reasonable price, they both agreed—they would need to find something to eat. Unprepared for the long ride, the last bite they ate was just before leaving on the trip, and both of their stomachs were now in desperate need of protein. They decided to continue east on Andrews Avenue, the only place where they could locate an array of traffic lights.

Something strange began to happen as they drove down this long stretch of road. Every business and home was either boarded up or was in the process of applying large sheets of wood onto all doors and windows. The workers seemed to be boarding as fast as they could go, as if they were in a hurry for some horrific event about to take place; portable saws and handfuls of nails being hammered down sounded somewhat like a construction site.

"Scott."

"Yes, honey."

"Did you hear anything about a hurricane coming this way?"

Scott actually didn't know how to respond to his wife's concern because he hadn't heard anything on the Weather Channel last night pertaining to a strong storm developing out in the Atlantic Ocean. Also, since they were from South Carolina, he was not surprised to see folks boarding up their homes this time of the year.

"This is so strange," Hazel managed to say with a puzzled look covering her face.

"Over there!" Scott shouted, startling his wife. He was pointing to an old man who could barely be seen as the large grill in front of him emitted clouds of smoke from items being cooked. The old man had a stand set up to sell food—hot dogs were a buck while burgers were two bucks—and fifty-cent shots of lemonade.

"I wonder why he didn't get the updated memo concerning the security of boarding up his place?" Hazel desperately wanted to know.

As Scott slowly turned the lemon into the lot where the old man was selling his products, two cars raced past him, the first one nearly smashing the lemon in the bumper. It was as if they were car racing for a prize at a finish line. But he and his wife just looked at each other as if to say, I guess they're running for cover.

"Howdy, folks," the old man said with a pleasant greeting. "I get it you're from out of town. That's all the business I've been getting over the last couple of hours."

The old man's back was slightly curved as he leaned over the grill. His clothes were clean, but the garments looked as though they were purchased years ago; the jeans were fading badly and the T-shirt had so many holes you could see gray hairs over the old man's chest. His grill looked as ragged as he did; the smoke from the grill seemed to not bother him at all.

"We *are* from out of town," Hazel answered from the passenger's seat of the car.

"Where is every one running off to?" Scott wanted to know.

The old man casually flipped a burger over, a cloud of smoke bursting off the grill in the process. "Well, let me ask you a question first: what brings you to this neck of the woods?" He immediately flipped another burger, which emitted another cloud of smoke, but this one sizzled loudly, unlike the first one, which was supposed to be meat as well.

"We're here on vacation," Hazel answered as she steadily got out of the lemon.

"On vacation? *In Henderson?*" For the first time, the old man looked curious.

"Yes, on vacation," Scott answered. He, too, was out of the lemon and was now walking toward his wife as she stood not too far from where he was now.

"To do what?" the old man demanded.

"To see the Vance Regional Botanical Garden," the couple answered simultaneously.

"Oh, I see. Those greenback crooks fooled you too!"

The couple looked surprised at one another. The noonday sun produced sweat that was now beaming down their foreheads as if they just got finished jogging, the temperature notching up a few degrees. Even though summer was about to fade away in a few weeks, the thermostat was still too high for this time of the year.

"Those who?" Scott investigated.

"Those bastards who run that garden," the old man said in a brusque tone of voice. "Every year they trick hundreds into coming here, but they never say a word about *them*!" The easy-going old man was now beginning to shout. He also raised his right hand while speaking as if this was some sort of protest gesture. "Look around, will you please! You think a city as ragged as this would have an attraction decent enough for folks from out of town to want to come and visit?! Hell, the only place I regularly go is right where you see me standing now, unless I hop up to the grocery store to find something on sale to fix on this here grill to make a few extra bucks!"

"Who is *them*?" Scott asked.

"Oh, I see. They got you folks really good!" He began to chuckle. "What I'm speaking of is those flying man-eaters. They're beautiful, but they're deadly!" He turned and pointed to a screened outdoor camper. "When they come, I just run in there and zip it up as tight as I can get it. They can see me—"

"Who *are* they?" Hazel interrupted.

The old man continued despite her interruption. "They can see me," he announced again, "but they can't get to my skin!" He sucked in as much oxygen as his old lungs could handle, all the while gently rubbing his scrawny forearms, which had rough-looking grayish-white hairs all over them.

"Who *are* they?" Scott shouted as if to be fussing at the old man.

"The butterflies!" the old man shouted back. "And you better hurry and take cover because it's about that time of the day for them to make an appearance!"

"Sorry, sir. I have a degree in botany. Even though I have mastered plants and the creatures that nest in them, then feed and gather nutrients from them, I know that butterflies don't bite. Actually, they only taste with their feet."

"Well, you're going to have a degree in economics once they start popping the crack of your ass and you see your doctor's bill!"

While the men were going back and forth, Hazel's stomach began to growl from the aroma the dogs and burgers emitted, no matter how ragged the old man's appearance looked. "Excuse me, sir. Could you kindly fix me up a dog and a burger, both with plenty of mustard and ketchup?" She already had the cost of three dollars tightly shut in her right hand, as if this were the last of the money she possessed.

But Scott was upset now. "No, honey. We can find food somewhere else," he hissed madly through his teeth.

"But dear, you noticed exactly what I have seen," she hungrily protested. "Everybody is closing up for the day."

The old man impolitely jumped in as loud as he could get. "Closing up for the day! No, they're closing up until late September!"

Scott grabbed his wife by her left arm, jerking her in anger toward him.

She disagreed with his unusual show of force, yanking freely away. "Do you know how long it's been since I last put food on my stomach?"

Scott was now pissed. He pushed the old man to the side and began fixing a bag of food for himself and his wife; a dog and a burger apiece. When he was finished he shouted, "Come on, honey! Let's get the hell out of here!"

"You'll be sorry for not listening!" the old man demanded as the couple jumped into the lemon, cranked the car up, and sped away.

They both look at the old man in disgust.

The old man pumped both fists into the air and shouted, "You'll be very sorry!"

Twenty minutes had passed by without a word spoken inside the lemon. But all the food was gone, including the smell, since Scott discarded the empty bag out the driver's side window and it landed clumsily onto Highway 85's hot pavement.

Hazel broke the silence by shaking her head and

telling the driver, "I can't believe you shoved that old man."

Laughter between the two.

"Then you had the nerve to fix us a free lunch. I knew there was something else I loved about you. I think you're so cute when you get angry." She sighed, then added, "But don't jerk my arm like that ever again. You hear?"

More laughter between the two.

"But you still enjoyed the food."

"Of course, I did. There's nothing like dogs and burgers on the grill during this particular holiday. Besides, I was hungry enough to eat a horse." She gently rubbed her stomach in satisfaction from the free meal.

Now the laughter was out of control.

"Let's just say we forget about the old man." He looked at the map instead of once again not using the cell phone's GPS system for directions, which was now atop the dashboard. "Pass me the map, will you. I need to pull over."

"For what?" she asked nosily.

"To find the hotel, honey." He sighed. "Listen, you know I don't go around hitting on people, right?"

She didn't answer, especially since he said to squash the whole situation.

"Right?"

She still did not answer.

"Okay. Let's just go to the hotel, take a hot shower,

relax a little, and then head to the garden. How about that?"

"What if that old man is telling the truth?" she asked worriedly.

"About what?"

"About the butterflies, Scott," she answered, staring coldly into his face.

"Honey," he said calmly, "butterflies don't bite. They taste with their feet."

"So why is this entire town freaking out?"

"Look at this place! Wouldn't you be freaked out?" He managed to gently rub her leg. "I mean, do any decent people live around here?"

"I'm serious, Scott," she said, at the same time pulling her leg away.

He turned on the radio and searched for a station, trying to ease the tension between them both. He mainly wanted to be nice to her just in case later on tonight he wanted to work on making a baby. It was now around one o'clock, and there was not one cloud in the sky to block out the blazing sun.

A few minutes later, Scott was pulling into the hotel's parking lot. Then, he turned off the radio, not interested in the old-school soul music a station called FOXY107 was banging into the lemon's stereo system.

"There is no way in hell that I will spend the night in that hotel!" Hazel shouted.

Scott hurriedly glanced back at the map to make sure he had the correct address. He shook his head to confirm that this was the correct address.

The hotel was only one bad storm away from collapsing; a few windows were missing from its eight-story red-brick frame. A black hearse was in the back of the hotel's right wing and was clearly visible. The car's windows were squeaky clean, shining brightly in the sunshine, and the paint job looked to be one that was recently completed, also shining brightly in the sunshine.

"Howdy, visitors," a voice spoke politely from the opposite side of the building.

"Who the hell are you?" Hazel interestingly asked.

"Calm down, young lady. I'm just trying to find cover. It's about time for *them*," he explained, pointing toward the other side of the hotel.

Scott wondered how many more strange people he would see while visiting Henderson.

Now Hazel was really pissed. "You mean to tell me that you dragged us both up here for this? And you actually charged this mess onto your credit card? I can't believe this!"

Scott could not muster a word. He wanted to turn the lemon around and head back home. He knew that there was no way to fix the events that have taken place over the past seventy minutes.

"I used to work here," the man said to break the ice.

He was tall and slim, and he wore black from the cap on his head to the shoes on his feet as if he were the driver of the hearse in the back of the hotel. His teeth were dingy black, completing his attire. "But this place closed down over two years ago." A polite inward laugh escaped his dingy mouth. "In the summertime, I hang around these parts for cover. Because they don't come around once the fall hits, which may be later than expected with all this heat." He looked shyly at his feet and continued, "Then I go back to staying in the woods over yonder."

Despite being mad beyond all means, Hazel found something to laugh about. The man's black attire reminded her of Herman Munster from the television show *The Munsters*. But that thought was definitely the only thing that was funny to her right about now.

Scott just stared at the hotel, thinking of how the folks who trick people into coming up here must be really cold-blooded. He decided that this place must be a crook's best-kept secret.

Hazel was not a big-breasted woman, but no one could tell by the way she stuck her chest out in anger. Her rhythmic breathing was strong and hard.

"Where are you guys from?" the man in black asked.

"South Carolina," Scott answered hoarsely; the couple wore Gamecock Polo shirts with matching blue jean shorts.

"How long have you guys been married?"

"Not too long to have a family, but to answer your question, we have been married for seven years," Scott answered.

"So, this is why you came to Henderson?"

"Apparently to see some dumb-ass garden!" Hazel replied.

"You mean the botanical garden? That piece of shit over yonder?" He pointed beyond where the black hearse currently sat. You could see yellow and orange flowers in the distance. You could also see a large dark hole, appearing to be a cave of some sort. "Why don't you guys get out of the car, stretch your legs a little."

"What is that darkness beyond the flowers?" Scott asked.

"Oh, that's a cave. Five thousand bats inside. And about a million butterflies."

"But butterflies don't live in caves," Scott demanded.

"Those bats do," the man in black replied. "Rumor has it the butterflies adapted a lot of bad habits from the bats, and now they live inside that cave with them. Sort of like one big strange family."

Scott and Hazel looked suspiciously at one another, trying to figure out if the man was trying to trick them both with some kind of spooky fairy tale, one with a scary ending, which may not surprise them in this town.

"I know this won't make any sense to either of you, but in the spring the bats fly back home from deep down south. You want to know why? Because this species doesn't like extremely cold weather but prefers to keep their bodies warm throughout the year."

The couple was still looking into each other's direction.

"Well, anyway," the man in black continued, "at the same time while they fly back home, caterpillars begin to crawl out of their cocoons up and down these surrounding tree branches." He pointed toward the trees nearest to the cave. "Well, at nighttime when the bats go out to catch moths, mosquitoes, and any other small creature they can snatch, their dung settles onto the branches where the caterpillars are crawling. Then, the caterpillars would eat the leaves the next morning, some containing small amounts of bat's dung attached to them. Then, when they develop to be butterflies, they also develop the characteristics, or should I say, the instincts of a bat."

The couple burst into laughter.

The man in black didn't quite get the joke.

Scott was just happy to be laughing because he felt that Hazel was no longer upset with him, despite the fact that this vacation was more or less ruined.

Hazel suddenly stopped laughing as the wind carried the awful scent of the man in black directly up to her nostrils.

Scott suddenly stopped laughing as he began to smell gas, knowing the lemon had probably lost most of the precious liquid he just pumped nearly ninety minutes ago.

"I guess Little Red Riding Hood lives just beyond the hotel and comes out at night with the bats!" Scott joked, forcing Hazel to burst out laughing again.

The man in black was still informative as he interrupted the laughter and continued to explain, "The daytime does not bother the butterflies because that's the environment they're used to."

But Scott could not finish without saying another joke. "So, what's your name? Is it Michael Myers? Or, let me guess, Jason?"

The couple once again burst out into laughter. This time, they had to lean against the lemon for balance to avoid tumbling down to the ground.

"Around here we call the butterflies daytime vampires," the man in black said in a stern and serious tone. His face looked as if his feelings were hurt from the couple's laughter.

Now, Hazel was feeling so much relief from her anger. "Let me ask you one question, sir. Why in the hell do you live way out here?" She was wiping tears from her eyes with either hand as she asked the question.

But the man in black was still very serious. "Mainly to hide from bill collectors, the cops, ignorant relatives, you name it." He fixed his eyes angrily onto Hazel. "After the butterflies descend from their daily flight, no one will come looking for you in these parts of the county." In his mind he was thinking, *Just you wait and see what's so funny*. Then he continued, "You have no idea how many people have been killed by those vicious butterflies."

The couple surveyed the surroundings, broad smiles covering either of their faces, apparently looking for any sign of human skeletal remains.

By now, all three were sweating continuously, especially the man in black, his attire absorbing the sun's rays the same way living bodies absorb food.

Now it was Scott's turn again. "Okay, mister, what do you want? Five dollars, a ride up the street, or some new clothes? Just name it and we will do our best to accommodate you."

Suddenly, all of the leaves on the surrounding trees took on all sorts of colors, distracting the couple from their shenanigans. A motley event that was so beautiful was currently taking place. The man in black, so upset that the couple did not show him any decorum, slipped into an unlocked door on this side of the hotel without making a sound.

"Look, Scott. They are so beautiful!"

"Yes, dear. If you don't move, one of them just might land on either of your shoulders or arms."

The man in black just found his usual hiding spot and stared out the window, which was far from any broken windows in the hotel. He had not seen the butterflies up close before, but he regularly sees devoured flesh of a human, a stray dog attacked, and has heard numerous stories about what the butterflies leave behind after taking flight, which is why he always goes for deep cover out of sight. Now he was interested to see what these creatures really do while searching for food.

"Ouch!" Hazel screamed as a beautiful yellowish-purple butterfly landed on her shoulder and bit her on the right hand when she reached out to make hand contact with the long and slender-bodied creature.

It was as if the rest of the butterflies could smell fresh blood as swarms of the creatures so beautiful in all sorts of fantastic color arrangements engulfed her in less than a minute. She frantically waved her arms into the air to avoid the attack, but that only seemed to entice them.

After looking around for cover, Scott managed to give the man in black one last look before he was attacked. He also managed one last thought about knowing that butterflies were diurnal non-meat eaters—*Are these insects biting my wife?*

The man in black couldn't see too much more of what he hoped to see, as the area turned temporarily dark from so many of the creatures flying out of the cave and into the open, blocking out the sun and casting a large, eerie-looking circular dark shadow. It was as if the bright yellow sun was not above. He thought it looked to be at least a million butterflies, the number he gave the couple earlier, but actually there were nearly three million of them living in the cave. The creatures made no sound, which actually made the event much more frightening.

Meanwhile, on the other side of town, thousands of butterflies were now landing onto buildings, trees, and cars. The old man with the grill stood silently inside his screened outdoor camper as the dwelling became covered with an assortment of beautiful butterflies. The creatures showed no interest toward the hotdogs and burgers still burning on the grill, but the smoke seemed to send a small portion of them into all sorts of chaotic directions, including atop the food. He wondered whether or not the young married couple from out of town made it inside to safety somewhere soon enough, other than that rundown thing called a car, oblivious to the fact that currently a large group of butterflies near a rundown hotel were having an out-of-town feast. But a small thought in the back of his mind whispered, *No, they didn't*. He knew then his thoughts were correct, especially since he was a long-time resident of this town and knew that any flesh left unprotected out in the open during the swarm would have no chance of surviving late June until the latter part of September.

He then sat down on an old chair inside the camper. A fly swatter lay at his feet, but he was not too pissed off enough to go swinging outside to save his food products.

Six hours later, the butterflies were back inside the cave.

The man in black had already confiscated the belongings of the married couple, which was only a few sets of clothes apiece from him and her, but one of the items included the lemon, which had parts that he maybe could sell for a few bucks at a local garage to last him financially for a couple of weeks. The sun was about an hour from beginning its setting into the western hemisphere. The day was beginning to cool off. Long shadows were casting from the woods where he stayed. He discarded the two bloody skeletons behind the hotel along with many others that lay in the back from previous carnivore events; he did this out of respect for human life.

Later on, he knew the other occupants of the cave— the bats—would be coming out to hunt. That's when he would normally find a place to sleep. He always slept peacefully despite his knowledge of the strange happenings every summer in this town: the butterflies will come out around one and go back into the cave after feasting just before the sun begins to set; after dusk, the bats would come out to hunt.

During the intervals of safety, he would take the same daily routine: find something to eat in the morning, hide in the early afternoon, go find something to eat again before the sun begins to set, then sleep peacefully at night. Just another ordinary summer's day in this strange town called Henderson.

Cries of the Little Children

The smell of new paint can be very strong, but at the same time highly satisfying. In this case, it meant a new place to start over again for Ava Kelt. She had just unloaded the last box out of her car and was now standing inside her new living room dead tired.

She opened the windows in front of her to allow some of the paint odor to escape while at the same time enjoying the smell of recently cut grass; once her nostrils became fixed on the paint odor, the smell of her belongings filled the air. The evening was a breezy low seventies, perfect weather for open windows.

Ava fished through the boxes on the floor to find the one that contained the nonperishable food items. Later on, since the smell of paint had now become bearable, she would prepare something for supper. But mainly all she wanted was a can of chicken noodle soup with plenty of saltine crackers, which would be something quick to prepare while at the same time not too heavy on a tired stomach; preparing a real meal would have to wait until tomorrow.

After locating supper, she desperately wanted to get upstairs and jump into the shower, her first shower in her new home. Her thirty-nine-year-old body needed to be rejuvenated by rushing hot water. Lately her body had begun to speak every once in a while, that it was feeling tired and needed proper rest. She knew that if the body does not get the rest it needs, it will force you to take a break. So, after moving all day, she was somewhat reluctant to go upstairs.

Once she finally made it up the stairs, she struggled to get out of her dirty clothes. She looked at the bathroom and for a short moment wished that she was finished showering and eating supper, and the only thing left to do was crash into bed. That's when she heard movement inside the bedroom closet.

One of the worst things any woman hates is mice, big or small. That's exactly what Ava saw when she cast a quick look inside the closet. Her body shivered all over. A female mouse was comfortably lying on her side nursing her five little pink children. She screamed to the top of her lungs and almost twisted her left ankle, at the last moment grabbing on to the bedpost to avoid a costly injury.

She ran into the bathroom to gather her thoughts. The shower and supper were the two furthest things from her mind at this very moment, even though her dirty body felt sticky and her stomach was growling. But she was not mad at the family inside her closet—she was upset because she earlier checked the entire house except for the closet inside her bedroom. If checked, she would have noticed the hole at the base of the closet door, which also extended outside of the window, with a small crack descending all the way to the house's foundation, which was probably part of the entrance for the mother rodent to enter and give birth. The setting sun shone directly on momma mouse, as if she were using its rays to stay warm, but actually resembled an actress on stage performing under a spotlight.

"Great!" Ava yelled. "My first day in my new house and I have a closet full of mice!"

But why didn't the painters notice the hole?

If they did, why didn't they say something?

Tired, hungry, and now pissed. All of this for a woman who was supposed to be enjoying her first night in her new home. All this and she just unpacked the last bag less than an hour ago.

During at least one of the trips while moving, she recalled seeing a giant yellow billboard sign with red letters stating: 1-800-GOT-MICE? Smaller letters near the bottom of the billboard stated that this particular group was the best at getting rid of rodents. Before taking the shower, she decided to give this business a call.

Now she became noxious to the fact that maybe she didn't check the entire place carefully. She thought, *What if there are more mice holes?* She continued to think silently. *Suppose that's why the house was so cheap in the first place? Because the house is filled with mice? Maybe I should have hired a professional inspector to do a thorough job for me before the purchase.* She knew that mistakes happened to people for trusting themselves with minimal knowledge about purchasing a product.

Within twenty minutes, the rodent exterminator was ringing the doorbell. Ava was still undressed. She had to yell out the bedroom window for the guy in the bright-red workman's outfit with a yellow baseball cap to wait a few minutes while she got dressed. To her, the man resembled a walking billboard. That thought produced laughter inside herself. He clearly looked to be someone who had the potential to exterminate rodents.

The guy's name was Zion; Ava was able to see on his left shirt pocket in small letters Zion Harris. He seemed to be nervous. Since he looked so young, and he announced himself as Zion, she still decided to just call him Mr. Harris.

"Well, ma'am," he spoke in a well-mannered tone, "I found a few more holes around the back up under the house. But I didn't find any more mice. I sealed up those three holes. Anyway, you shouldn't have any more problems."

She quickly remembered that she left her bright-colored pink panties on the bedroom floor, forgetting to throw them to the other side of the bed out of sight while hurrying to get dressed. She knew for a fact that if he removed the rodent family out of the bedroom closet, he most definitely noticed her panties on the floor near the closet door. She thought silently again, *Is this why the young man seemed so nervous?*

She rushed into the kitchen and found her purse on the kitchen counter and was excited that Mr. Harris's company accepted checks, especially in a world where swiping a debit or credit card was becoming more of a way of payment. She wrote the check out for ten dollars more than the bill, thanking the young man first for coming so quickly and second for finding the other holes.

"By the way," he said while walking to the bright red-and-yellow company truck, "I like the landscaping out here on your front lawn. It will surely receive a lot of positive remarks."

She had no idea as to what he was talking about, especially since the only landscaping on the front lawn was a yard previously cut. She thought, *He did see my panties, and he liked them. That statement was just made to throw me off!*

Back upstairs, with the fear of mice over, she knew the shower would come at this very moment, the supper right after, and the bedroom would immediately follow, no matter if folks say you need to stay up awhile after eating a meal.

Ava felt very relaxed after showering and eating supper. The soup and crackers hit the hunger pain head on, hard enough to the point that she became unaware of the rodent problem.

However, the light overhead was becoming quite discomforting. Not only was it keeping her awake, but the brightness burned her tired eyes. But before turning the source of light off, she would first head downstairs to make sure all the doors and windows were secured and locked.

On her way back upstairs, she thought she heard laughter coming from the kitchen. After pausing for a moment, knowing that her mind and body were exhausted and that she thought that laughter was coming from the kitchen area, she continued upward to bed.

Once she was inside the bedroom—the master bedroom—she heard the laughter again, only this time the noise was muffled, as if from a distance. She sighed when out of the corner of her left eye she saw a few kids playing in the street. But she knew that sleep must come soon because the kids seemed to be skipping in rhythm in slow motion. Also, their feet seemed to be at least six inches from the pavement. She was in a trance watching them, as if her vision were quiescent at seeing the children; she couldn't exactly make out how many kids were actually playing in the street.

She snapped out of her trance as her eyes rolled to a large object in the yard in view, right under the bedroom window. Even though the sun was casting a pinkish and somewhat purplish glow over a group of cumulus clouds, she still couldn't make out exactly what the object was.

Ava dreaded going back downstairs, which was now completely dark. Her right foot clumsily kicked an unpacked box that she didn't remember putting there in the first place, which was near the front entrance door. Without shoes on, her foot began to dance to the rhythm of her heartbeat.

She opened the door and walked quickly toward the side of the house. The aroma of fresh earth was all around, as if dirt was recently dug into. Up close, the figure under her bedroom window resembled an effigy used for punishing those who had bad intentions, the only difference was an extreme height of nearly ten feet tall, which is probably why she was able to see part of the figure from upstairs.

As she turned to hurry back into the house, she was surprised as to how big her new dwelling seemed. Maybe it was the rush of fear that encircled her mind that her dwelling resembled the big white house in the *Amityville Horror* movies.

Now finally back inside, and panting heavily, she

paused before picking up her cell to dial 9-1-1. What explanation could she give to the authorities? Someone just recently dug up a giant stickman at the side of her house? And you didn't even notice anyone digging?

Now she remembered what rodent-man had said earlier concerning her lawn, about complimenting her landscaping. She dropped her cell phone, knowing that the operator would have a great time explaining this strange call to her coworkers.

She gathered herself together and turned on the light near the entrance to the house. With the blinds wide open she could see the midsection of the figure just outside the kitchen window. The caramel coloring on the figure's backside she decided was dirt.

The figure bent over, glanced through the kitchen window, and smiled two rows of missing and yellowed teeth. But she still wondered if all she needed to do was go to bed and get some sleep.

Enough of being frightened. She rushed back outside and stomped around to the side of the house. Once there, she kicked the stickman and was surprised at how easily he tumbled down toward the grass, especially since he seemed to be lively just moments earlier. Even though this was the first house for her to not rent, she was already ambivalent toward the fact that someone has been messing with her lawn.

After stacking the wood of the figure about a foot

from the road, careful not to block the driveway, Ava went back inside her dwelling, brushing earth off the front of her fresh white T-shirt, meaning that she was now dirty again. She decided that after changing clothes again, the first thing on the agenda in the morning would be to start life fresh all over, since she would be waking up in her new home for the very first time.

Dylan Rowen was now accustomed to sleeping with his bedroom light on at night, normally around this time of the year. Too many bad incidents seemed to take place after the happenings inside that big white house up the street just a couple of years ago.

He used to love all those kids whom lived in that big white house. To him, all ten of them were adorable. But he hated the family that took them in as foster children. He regularly wondered over and over again how the state could let a family with a known history of the occult deep inside their genes adopt so many adorable and precious-looking kids. Seven girls and three boys would seem to be a lot, but he figured that the family needed that many kids to pay for such a gigantic house.

Concerning the house: now he couldn't figure out why a single lady with no kids would want such a big house to live in all by herself. Unless she was planning on starting a large family sometime in the near future.

He clearly remembered the first night the screams

came from that house. His beloved dog, Bo, mysteriously wanted to go for a walk at half-past midnight nearly two years ago. There was a full moon shining brightly overhead on a clear and cool night. The wind rustled a few dead leaves up and down the quiet streets and sidewalks. All sorts of aromas were carried on the wind: dead leaves, some type of stew, freshly cut grass, and caked oil on dry streets. While Bo sniffed into the direction of where the stew was roasting from, Dylan felt that someone must be like him, up at night and unable to go to sleep.

Again, this was an aberrant way for Bo to act. The golden retriever's coat glowed under the light from the full moon. Then, after about a three-minute walk around the block, they came up to where the big white house sat. Bo began to groan, something the dog never did before. The noises in that silent night were those demonic parents yelling and screaming at those precious little kids. The question entered his mind as to why the kids were up so late in the first place, especially on a school night?

George and Judy Ovum were their names. The guardians were just screaming at the top of their lungs. "Say it! Sticks and stones may break my bones, but words will never hurt me! Say it!"

What followed the screaming was the sound of loud pops, as if someone was being whipped by a belt made of genuine leather.

Then the kids began to cry.

After that night, Dylan occasionally walked Bo close to midnight and sometimes in the daytime, as long as weather permitted, slowing their paces once they were in front of the Ovum residence. He knew a call to Child Support Enforcement would be appropriate to the sounds coming from that big white house. *Sad thing all those kids died in that house,* he always regretfully thought to himself every night after their deaths. But he was just like any other fearful law-abiding citizen, which meant that he just kept to himself. Tonight, as he prepared to walk Bo, he wondered if he should warn the little lady who just moved in, about what took place in that house just a couple of years ago around this time of the year.

A good night's sleep was just the perfect prescription a doctor will give for a tired body that's been moving, loading, and unloading furniture, suitcases, bags, and boxes for the past couple of days. Ava awoke to a comforting morning stretch, her aching muscles relaxing in the process. She glanced over at the alarm clock on the nightstand and was pleased that she had just slept until 11:30 a.m. Fridays were always one of her best days. For her, the day meant she didn't have to work tomorrow. Plus, this particular Friday fell on the two-week payday. Now her vacation would be much sweeter with money in her pocket. But she knew that unpacking that last box downstairs was just as important as anything else. Worshipping her pillow would now have to wait until later on tonight.

As soon as she pulled the covers off her rested body, she began to hear the laughter again. Her memory quickly flashed back to last night.

A loud jet flying overhead drowned out the laughter.

Once the jet was at a distance, laughter again.

Coming from up the hall in one of the three empty bedrooms.

Now the sound of one of the bedroom doors shrilling loudly on its hinges.

Ava sat up in bed, her face stunned. One of her worst fears came after watching the paranormal series on the Sci-Fi Channel, but she assumed the show was not real, just a bunch of special effects mess. She had also watched a couple of the *Paranormal Activity* horror flicks on DVD. But she figured that the movies were just as fake as the television episodes.

Since the blinds were tightly drawn, only a small amount of light shone upstairs. She sat at the edge of the bed and listened attentively. She became frustrated when a loud car went by, playing some rap song loud enough to make the walls of the house shake, distracting her concentration.

Ava peeped out the blinds once she was on her feet. She wished the golden retriever would just shut up, barking loudly at her house as if he were insane. And why was the owner of the dog doing nothing but staring at the house like someone waiting for a peep show to get started?

A loud crash from one of the bedrooms.

The dog was now barking frantically.

Another round of laughter.

A stream of fear suddenly rushed through Ava.

Her cell phone began to ring, scaring the living daylights out of her. She did not recognize the number so she just allowed her phone to continue to ring, which meant that if it was important they would leave a message.

As she stepped out of the bedroom to investigate the strange noises, the hallway seemed to stretch a mile long. A large part of her was fearful at what she might see.

First bedroom on the left. Empty. No movement or sound.

Second bedroom on the right past the stairs. Empty. No movement or sound.

Third bedroom at the end of the long hallway on the left. Before getting to this bedroom, she knew that this had to be the one where the noises were coming from. She approached the bedroom door with caution, wondering why she was beginning to fear her new house after living here less than a full day. But she was still brave enough to not think of carrying any protective device in either hand.

As she glanced into the bedroom, the first thing she saw was the bed, which was still not set up. The mattresses and boards leaned restlessly against the wall just the way she left them; she wished they didn't cover the window, blocking light that would come in handy right about now. But she was in no hurry to set up the bed because this room was quickly designated as a guest bedroom weeks ago. When she glanced to the left—behind the door—she was aghast at what she saw; a large stack of dolls lay on the floor at the foot of the opened closet door. These were not just any dolls. They all seemed to look alive to Ava, not with that plastic glow that fake dolls are supposed to have. She could clearly see this illusion, even in the dim light. So she hit the light switch near the door. She quickly covered her mouth with both her hands when she noticed all the bruises covering the dolls' faces and arms. Where the dolls came from, she hadn't the slightest idea.

She was now so frightened that she almost ran downstairs and out of the house into the front lawn. As a child, she used to always run from those who regularly picked on her. But one day her mother explained that just because she had a petite frame and would probably receive harsh treatment for years to come, sometimes you have to just stand up and fight for yourself without running. And that's what she decided to do right now—only she had no idea what to stand up for.

This was all crazy to Ava. She had no idea about what to do next. The only thing she could think of was deciding to be apprehensive about staying inside the house any longer, especially by herself, even though she just moved in. She was totally off balance from the recent events inside her new home.

As she looked down the hallway to make sure nothing would be able to creep up from behind, she worriedly glanced at herself in the mirror of the bathroom. Even though she smiled at herself, she recognized her dark-eyed and terrified appearance.

She went over to the bed, pushing the contents to the side to allow room to open the blinds and then the window. As she did so, a large bug flew against the window, which was followed by a black crow doing the same, apparently chasing down a noonday meal. As she glanced through the window, the house across the street had two front windows that resembled a set of sad eyes, particularly the way the blinds were only pulled a few inches up.

The dolls were mysteriously gone!

Were they there in the first place?

Maybe something bad was about to happen?

Ava blinked her eyes a few times to insure herself that nothing was in front of the closet. She walked over to the closet, knelt down, and waved her right hand in the spot where the dolls just recently lay, ensuring herself that nothing was there.

She looked deep inside the closet to make sure that no mice had made a home. The way things were going lately, she probably would not be surprised if *two* families of mice had made this closet their new home.

For some reason, she began to miss work. Just last week she was so excited to plan a vacation in order to have all the time she needed to move. Now she wanted to put her new home into the back of her mind. Taking around a hundred calls a day to verify insurance policies was stressful before the vacation, but now she wished that she was back at the office.

Her stomach began to growl. After eating lightly last night, her body needed some fuel. Even though this Friday was now a melancholy day for her, she still needed to eat.

Dylan could only come up with one explanation: the new girl must be from out of town. How the hell did she not know what went on in that house? It was the biggest story on the news for nearly a month! Was she living under a rock before she purchased the house?

"Go get me that remote, Bo," he ordered. The only thing he wanted to do was watch television, the life of someone who is receiving disability and unable to work. "Good job, Bo," he said while brushing the dog's hair out of place over the head.

He always watched the news after giving Bo his late-morning walk. But today's news caught him off guard. He learned that jury selection for the upcoming trial for the Ovums was to take place this evening at the downtown courthouse.

"Well, I'll be damned!" he spoke to no one in particular, even though Bo's ears jerked up and down. "Just what I need to see!"

He was excited enough to roll up the sleeves on his shirt. Blood vessels stood out on his scrawny arms. The wiry black hairs on his forearms looked exactly like the hairs on his head.

"Bo," he called to his dog. Now he was talking to someone. "I hope those bastards get what they deserve!"

Bo didn't quite understand too much English except the commands he learned as a puppy. So he decided to just lay on the carpet in front of the television, his head buried underneath his front paws; his owner had no idea that the dog was actually thinking about the strange mess going on up the road at that big white house.

Dylan wished he had the young lady's name and phone number so that he could call and explain to her that something important was on the noonday news. He decided that later on today—without Bo accompanying him—he would knock on her front door. But first he would stop by the convenience store up the street to see if the story had made the papers the same way it had made the noonday news.

Ava felt trapped inside the house with the rest of the blinds shut, making the house seem cluttered. She sighed, then began to open all the blinds inside the house one by one, the sun's rays bursting through in gigantic blocks as she did so.

First, she opened the blinds in the living room. It seemed to take forever just to open the three of them. The house across the street still had windows that resembled sleepy eyes. While she focused on the house's windows, she wondered if they were experiencing the same strange problems as she was now having.

Now she was inside the kitchen. There were only two blinds in this area: one over the sink and another in the dining room area. On this side of the house she marveled at the other gigantic homes throughout the neighborhood.

For some reason, she glanced into the sink and thought of how she always kept dirty dishes in her apartment. Then she figured that it wouldn't take long before she would have the same lazy problem in this sink.

When she looked up from the sink, she was livid. Through the window she saw the same bogey from last evening, except the figure was at the corner of the house. A giant stickman dressed with the same attire Ava loved to wear with loose clothing, smiling at her the same way it did last evening. Plus, she knew for sure this pile of mess was supposed to be at the edge of the street to be picked up as trash. No need to think that the neighbors were playing a devious trick with her, even though she remembered the kids playing in the street last evening.

Out of her peripheral vision she thought she saw the blinds move outward in the master bedroom upstairs. Or was the vision just one of the approaching cumulus clouds blocking out the early evening sun?

The noises from upstairs again.

Panic from within Ava's body.

The noises drifted into a cadence like a church choir at the end of a song.

Ava thought, *I am standing in my kitchen in my new home in the middle of the day hallucinating about dolls, a stickman, children singing, and sad eyes in windows. Or am I being mendacious about what's* really *going on?*

While she was thinking to herself, a strong hand grabbed her right shoulder from behind, causing her to almost faint.

Ava and Dylan talked for hours. In the sky over-head, the sun was just beginning to set, casting a pur-plish-orange outline around the few remaining clouds as they hurriedly passed by. The first crickets began to chirp. Through the living room window she noticed a few skippers darting in fast flight around the street lights, but if only she knew, they normally do jerky motions of flight in the daytime; maybe it was best she didn't know.

"I tell you, honey, those people were crazy," Dylan continued to explain, his words carefully enunciated. He squeezed his hat as a sign that he was anxiously wanting to go.

"I just don't recall hearing any of this."

"Well," Dylan continued, "with so much stuff going on in this world these days, it's hard to keep up with all the latest news."

"And why did you say the parents did all of this foolishness? The foster parents, I mean."

Dylan desperately wanted to get back to Bo, whom he decided at the last minute to keep at home, but he answered by adding, "Well, the kids got picked on a lot in school for being foster kids. You know how kids are these days—always trying to find a reason to intimidate one another around. But when the kids came home to explain themselves, that's when everything would start. Sometimes lasting into the wee hours of the morning."

"I bet that was so awful on those poor little kids."

"I used to listen to them," he went on, but only for this last time. "They used to shout at the kids before beating them. I can't forget those screams. They would yell at them, 'Sticks and stones may break my bones, but words will never hurt me!'"

Ava shook her head in disgust.

Dylan saw this as a perfect moment to just get up.

Ava didn't even notice his movement.

"Be sure to keep up with the evening news," he added before heading toward the front door.

As she got up to show him out, she asked, "And what did they call those murders?"

"The *Charlotte Observer* headlined them as, 'The Adopted Killers.' Any time you read or hear about this—that's those bastards! Hopefully they will burn in hell!" Finally he warned her, "If you hear my dog barking, I think he can sense something supernatural going on inside this house."

Ava had already figured that one out after the commotion this morning. She also knew that the excitement generated from finding a place to live and finally moving kept her out of the news for a while. She wished Dylan a good night and watched him walk down the street until he was out of sight.

Once she sat down, the visit by Dylan was so concerning to her. Also, it was pleasing to her how he took the time to visit a total stranger to get her up to date about her new living quarters.

Something supernatural going on inside the house? That's when she recalled seeing the stickman twice; even though he was outside, that was still considered close enough. Had Dylan seen anything supernatural going on at the house? *Even before I moved in? Did he happen to see the stickman and thought it was a decoration the same way rodent man thought it was great landscaping?*

Her stomach began to growl again. She was now weak in the knees and in need of some serious energy from any form of protein, especially after surviving on a can of soup for nearly a full day. A can of Beanee Weenee would have to do for now. Maybe a peanut butter and jelly sandwich just before bed. But anything before she just passes out onto the floor.

After eating, she knew that a tough decision would have to be made. With everything that had been happening in and around the house, she thought of not sleeping here tonight. But she couldn't think of where to go. She definitely did not want to see if Dylan had an extra bed, especially since they just met this afternoon. Calling a friend or relative was also off limits as well, because all they would want to know is, "What's wrong with the house?"

Once her stomach was filled, she just sat downstairs on the couch. The peace was comforting. Her thoughts were not distracted by some paranormal incident. Just staring at the walls. Staring for nearly thirty minutes. That's when she noticed what looked like a blur of words coming through the white paint on the wall just above the flat-screen television. As she turned to look at the other freshly painted walls in the living room, she noticed the same thing.

Now she really became spooked. Three weeks ago she was at the Home Depot in the university side of north Charlotte looking for a hammer and nails to hang pictures on the walls. A paint scrapper caught her attention because a large box contained many of them, which were advertised to be 50 percent off. After a thorough inspection of the house, and noticing a few more blurred words, the paint scraper was exactly what she needed at this very moment.

She carefully began removing paint wherever she saw blurred words. Atop the television was a likely start, since that's where she first noticed the words. Since the house was recently painted she had little problem removing the white substance, peeling carefully as she scraped. As the paint peeled off so easily, she knew it had to be a cheap brand. The first word she made out was NEVER. By the time she removed the paint off the entire wall, a sentence read: STICKS AND STONES MAY BREAK MY BONES, then beneath that, BUT WORDS WILL NEVER HURT ME! Close to an hour later, the same words were written on two other walls upstairs. All three phrases were written in red letters—she almost cried at the thought that they were written in the children's blood. She realized that the words were difficult to see when she visited the house prior to moving in because the paint was still drying. She desperately wanted to go throughout the neighborhood to find where Dylan lived.

That's when she heard a dog barking. But when she peeped through the blinds, Bo was not with Dylan. The dog barked as if he were recently assigned to protect Ava.

Now she remembered the stickman at the side of the house, thinking the dog may be barking at it. But when she glanced to the left of the house, the stickman was gone; his wooden frame was not at the curbside either.

What could he possibly be barking at? she wondered.

She decided to go outside and quickly make friends with Bo, because by now she felt that the dog knew who she was. The closer she got to the dog, the more he marched into the direction his owner traveled earlier after paying her a visit. She felt safe following Bo, plus she had an instinct that something may be wrong with Dylan, knowing that the dog was not trying to get her attention because something was happening inside the house, as Bo had done earlier.

Nearly a block away, Ava glanced back at her new home, reciting inside her mine the strange happenings and the writings on the walls. The house's spookiness was elevated as she saw the blinds in her master bedroom tremble, as if the spirits of darkness were warning her to never come back, which at the present moment seemed like a great idea.

The dog's pace quickened the farther they were away from her house.

After another fifty yards she glanced back again.

Bo stopped dead in his tracks to wait for Ava when their distance increased.

Up ahead she could see a gathering of folks. Even though she didn't know they were her neighbors, she was interested as to why so many folks were gathered together right in the middle of the street.

Sirens were blaring in the distance. At that moment, she had no idea that they were headed in the same direction that Bo was trying to lead her.

It was difficult to see over so many people at the back of the crowd. As Bo made a clear path for her leading up to the front door of this particular house, she knew that this was the residence of Dylan. The crowd parted as if the dog was someone with authority.

"Oh my God!" someone from the crowd frantically spoke.

Oohs and ahhs followed that statement.

When Ava saw Dylan attached tightly to the stick-man, looking as if he was participating in some sort of crucifixion, his scrawny body covered in blood, she almost fainted. His head drooped down as if he was admiring his blood-soaked body. While the crowd and the authorities had no idea as to what was happening, she clearly knew. She wondered if he took some sort of spirit home with him after visiting her house. She also wondered how bad her credit would be after defaulting on a mortgage after only a little over a day of living in her new residence.

Months had gone by, and Ava still had not mentioned a word about what happened that horrifying night at Dylan's residence to anyone she knew. All she wanted to do was move on in life, to just pick up the pieces and start all over again, even though the hand she was dealt had a very short and horrifying time frame.

She was extremely happy with the new apartment. Bo seemed to enjoy his new residence, as well. She felt that even though the dog was happy, he knew a little about what happened to his owner. She just wished that she could've seen the terror coming.

She made sure to leave the house in ruins, mainly to make sure that no one else would have to live through the same experience as she did, or by the time they fixed the place up it would take a while, and that might just disturb what was fearing her inside the house. With a promotion at work, she would be able to pay for the apartment, save some extra cash, and one day start the home-buying journey all over again, even though her credit at the moment was trashed. But she would be a bit more cautious the second time around if she ever decided to purchase a piece of property again.

The only thing she was upset with was the fact that with Dylan gone no one would be able to testify against the Ovums. This thought highly pissed her off. She knew the couple would not get the punishment they deserved. She figured that the couple would still live in Charlotte once they beat the case, and for what happened to those kids and to Dylan, she one day hoped that they could be found. If she managed to find them, the semiautomatic handgun she purchased this morning would serve justice once and for all.

Zombie Love

Love can be described very simply: I'll do anything for you!

That was the continuous thought going through Rosa's mind as she paced the living room floor back and forth for nearly two hours. The death of her husband caught her—and everyone else close to this family—by surprise. He just passed out and died, with no traits of an illness and no complaints of sickness. Even though a considerable amount of tension was on her mind, the expression on her face was rather stolid.

She paced the floor for a reason other than her husband's death. She recalled hearing nearly a year ago a Spanish rumor about a professional worker of magic from a primitive South American society now living in the United States who specialized in bringing the recently dead back to life. Even though Rosa had no concrete evidence that the rumor was true, she was willing to go to the extreme to see her husband alive again. She also knew that this particular person was not far from where she currently stayed, which the gossipers of the rumor pronounced. Very soon, self-motivation would lead her to this person's place of residence.

She finally sat down from tiredness. As she looked fixedly at the romantic photos of her small family on the surrounding walls, her mind raced at past thoughts of the moments she and Warren previously shared. The first time she laid eyes on him, and he gave her the same look, her heart was immediately stolen. He stole her heart, which is why she's so sorrowful they didn't have a child together, which would have been her second love. Other guys from her past romantic and short-lived life were just someone to date, to escape a feeling of loneness. But not her dead husband. She thought of how he would squeeze her shoulders before kissing her, how he would laugh at anything she joked about, how handsome he was, how well he dressed, and how great he used to make love to her. He was her perfect gentleman.

When her thoughts slowed to an acceptable pace, she was aware of how important it would be to see her former lover face-to-face again. First thing tomorrow morning she decided to go pay this so-called worker of magic a special visit, to see if there was such a thing as conjuring someone back from the dead, no matter what consequences she would have to face later on in life.

The light of the sun was barely visible over the eastern

horizon, and all the surroundings were still blanketed in darkness, especially since there were not too many street-lights in the area. The neighboring trees resembled tall dark statues. What was supposed to be an open field of grass looked more like a large mass of nothing. Rosa wanted to get an early start to only be seen by as few individuals as possible, to save time from speaking and conversations about subjects she knew that today wouldn't be too interesting. She was actually too embarrassed to let anyone know her plans for the day.

After intently searching the internet most of yesterday for the magic worker's place of business—she was amazed that information like this was available on the net in such full detail—finding the nearby location would be simple. All she needed to do was locate Winter Grove Pond, find the multitude of hornets' nests adjacent to a group of willow trees to the right of the pond, walk as straight as an arrow for about a mile, turn left at the BEWARE OF QUICKSAND sign, look for another set of older trees at the edge of an approaching forest—which would contain deadly poison ivy climbing left to right up most of their bark—and the magic worker's house would be hidden behind this area. The web page's site explained that the upward growth of the poison ivy's sticky leaves up the older trees was still a mystery to scientists, which actually gave Rosa the confidence that something magical may actually take place in the area.

Rosa nearly fainted as a large group of cardinal birds suddenly began to sing loudly as if welcoming the upcoming sunrise. She was only startled because of her deep concentration of the adventurous job ahead of her.

Finding Winter Grove Pond was no problem for her. The fish in the pond were gulping for air, and the noise they made splattering the water startled her again. For a quick moment, she recalled seeing numerous people coming back from this same pond with fresh food to eat, mostly consisting of small brim and large black bass, but they occasionally had heaps of them.

With the first part of her journey complete, she continued.

Up ahead was an array of trees. But it was very difficult to spot the willows covered with the deadly insects, since the light of the sun only brightened objects in the distance where it rose bright and yellow. She mainly wanted to keep away from the hornets' deadly stings, even though she had no idea if they would be active or not in the dark.

She stood still, cautiously looking around in the dark for any signs of danger approaching, because she really didn't know how to proceed at the moment.

After a few moments, the sky began to brighten, the surroundings resembling dusk. The surrounding trees no longer resembled tall dark statues, neither did the grass look like a gigantic dark mass of nothing. Her eyes fixed on a group of large willow trees about forty feet tall; she was naïve to the fact that this particular species of tree could produce aspirin. She knew that these were the trees she was looking for because she didn't see any other trees that resembled them. She could also make out large circles around the base of each tree, even though the branches with numerous leaves dangled lowly, which must be the nests of the deadly hornets. She had to contain herself by the size of the nests. Once she was close to the trees, she noticed that they were twisted badly near the top. She wondered if the trees were twisted because of the huge nests latched onto them, or if this was a sign not to fool around on the magic worker's property, as if to say entering through here is the exact same as entering at your own risk into somewhere you may hate you ever visited in the first place.

She was so thankful now as the cloudless sky quickly became brighter from the oncoming sunrise. Mainly she was thankful because she knew that if not careful, a sting from a hornet would stop her journey in its tracks, and with no one close around, that could be a deadly situation for her. As she passed through the willows, all the other surrounding trees began to sway back and forth, as if the magic worker had his own version of nature's special effects system. The trees rhythmically seemed to want to grab her and keep her for their own personal endeavors. This eye-popping experience would be one that she would not soon forget.

For the next mile, with the aid of now full brightness,

Rosa walked to her own rhythm, occasionally watching out for danger once again by paying attention to either side of her and from behind. She knew that a woman walking by herself to a place that seemed to be out in the middle of nowhere could immediately change into a terrible situation.

She stopped to gather herself and take a drink of water from a half-empty bottle that was now warm from being clutched tightly in her right hand. But she quickly became well-rested when she saw the sign warning of quicksand.

She cautiously walked to the area where the sign was located. Once she got to the area where the earth was moist and loose, she stopped dead in her tracks. She wondered if the smell coming from the quicksand may be because something with blood had died at the bottom of its pit. Even though the smell was worse than sewage, at the same time, the smell was as sweet as cinnamon. The combination of aromas almost made her breakfast threaten to disgorge from her stomach. Instead of vomiting, she first drank the remaining hot liquid, tossed to plastic bottle over her shoulder, quickly walked a huge circle around the quicksand area, and continued on her journey for what she expected should not be too long of a distance.

Just up ahead, Rosa noticed another set of very large trees. She really didn't know too much about poison ivy, but the dark green leaves growing strangely from the ground up the bark of the few trees directly in front of her was enough to convince her that, after nearly a two-hour journey, and the heat of the sun now beaming down through a few open areas of the forested area, she was finally at her destination.

She stood as still as the large trees surrounding her. What was puzzling to her was the fact that she hadn't seen a bug, a reptile, or even a bird this deep in the forest. But she was now no longer afraid of her surroundings.

"Who goes there?" The baritone voice came from behind the poison ivy encrusted trees.

The voice surprisingly did not startle Rosa. She actually gained more bravery knowing that someone was close by in these spooky surroundings. She felt that the magic worker may have some powerful remedies after all, even though a small part of her was convincing enough to otherwise make her feel that the trip would just be a waste of time. Besides, her mother always taught her not to trust anyone you didn't know, and all she knew about the magic worker was a rumor.

"I said, who goes there?" This time the magic worker shouted.

"M...M...My name is Rosa. Rosa Pinkston." Her childlike response was only due to the fact that she didn't want the magic worker upset at her early-morning visit.

"What brings you to these parts?"

"Well...." She began to wonder if he was upset, and if it would've been best to just wait a few hours before planning the trip.

"Come closer!" His shouting now seemed to echo through the silent surroundings.

"I came because..." Rosa couldn't believe that she came this far just to choke up her words deep inside the depths of her throat. She smacked her lips in disgust. The green surroundings seemed to be closing in around her, causing a feeling of isolation; the magic worker's deep voice didn't aide in her feeling any better.

After a brief period of silence, he yelled, "What brings you here?"

Rosa sighed deeply and gathered herself together. She noticed how difficult it was now for the sun's rays to shine through the thick vegetation with everything closing in. "I came because..." She wondered if the liquid running down her legs was this morning's orange juice or sweat from anxiety. "I heard that you..."

Were the trees now laughing at her?

"I heard that you can bring someone back from the dead."

The trees *were* laughing at her!

The magic worker remained silent, at least to try and understand the woman on his property.

"I want to know if you can assist me in bringing my dead husband back from the grave," she finished explaining, not wanting to sound silly.

On the other end was more silence.

Rosa felt relieved to finally get her words together.

Still there was no response from the magic worker.

Now Rosa really felt that the trip was not worth her time.

A rustling of vegetation whispered from beyond the trees.

The odor seemed to be coming back from the quicksand, at the same time forcing her to swallow deeply to avoid gagging up her breakfast, again!

Then a small man entered into the opening.

Rosa looked the man up and down as if to bring him back from resuscitation. Not only did he look unpleasant, but he was only three feet tall. Her mouth was agape in shock, especially from listening to his baritone voice. *No way could this be the man I was just talking to,* she thought. She felt as if she was being vigilant for no apparent reason.

"I may be able to help you," he said confidently.

"How much would your services cost?"

"My services to you will be for free. Why? Because I'm only going to tell *you* what to do." He glanced at the surrounding trees. "How long has your husband been dead?"

"Well, only three days." She now felt at ease to talk. "But we had a quick burial, so he's six feet under now."

"Very good," he replied politely. "That means we still have time."

Rosa began to blush from the fortunate news, even though she was still puzzled at the magic worker's appearance. But after seeing the magical events happening all around her, she felt that this guy must know *something*. She didn't even bother to question him as to why his voice was not so intense and strong while talking in the open area.

"Here's what you have to do. First, I don't want you to tell anyone about this visit, even though a lot of folks already know that I exist, but most is just gossip, not a known reality. Second, the trees around you are very powerful. If you are not a slow person, you can see that the leaves are turning blue as they warm in the morning sunrise, which means that you must realize that they have some type of magical intent."

Rosa fixed her gaze on the tree closest to her right, noticing that the leaves close to the top were already turning blue, but she had no idea what type of tree it was, or how it could still flourish with so much poison ivy fastened onto it. She became curious as to what the leaves have to do with bringing her three-day-old dead husband back to life.

The magic worker inched closer to where she was, close enough for her to smell the aroma of cinnamon coming from off his clothing, which puzzled her even more. *Why would a magic worker smell like fresh cinnamon?* She thought.

"You take three of the leaves, which have already turned blue, and tuck them gently under your shirt. You must not let the heat from the sun dry these leaves of their precious nutrients. As soon as possible, get to your husband's grave, pierce any part of your body, and next, carefully sprinkle drops of your blood until the leaves are thoroughly covered. Then, dig at least three feet deep over his grave, lay the blood-soaked leaves on top, and gently cover the burial with the loose dirt."

"Why would I want to sprinkle my blood onto the leaves?"

"The ritual is different when a married or long-term relationship partner is involved. Since it's your husband, when the leaves awaken him, he will know the scent of your blood, enabling him the follow the scent to the owner."

"But…"

"No buts. You must act quickly. Three days is the limit. And don't tell anyone you came to see me. Not anyone!"

Rosa did not think of returning to her humble abode after leaving the magic worker. She just hoped that no one saw her entering or leaving Elmwood Cemetery. Besides, her window of opportunity was closing fast because the cemetery was approximately four miles from the magic worker's place of residence, she didn't own a car, and she did not have time to wait until dark.

How he would be able to crawl out of a coffin under six feet of earth meant that this must be some type of magic! But she insisted on following the instructions from the small man with the strange voice.

Her jeans contained moisture around the right thigh where she pierced herself. But she was not bleeding too badly; the spot was only an inch in diameter. The sight of the spot threw her equilibrium off balance, afraid of the thought of bleeding to death. Courage kept her going by reminding her how bad she wanted to see her dead husband again.

Once home, and after the wound stopped bleeding, she sat on the bed naked and wondered how decomposed Warren's body would be, after the embalming and burial. With this thought on her mind, she lay down and drifted off to sleep, the evening sun shining through the bedroom window onto her caramel-brown face.

A few moments later, she was still half asleep after sitting up in bed. It was difficult for her to gather her brain into full function and her eyesight into focus in the dark room.

Once her thinking was clear, and she was able to make out objects, she turned on the light by the bedside and walked over to the dresser to get her nightgown; even though the daytime temperature was close to ninety, the air became cool at night. The pain in her thigh was the only thing that reminded her about this morning's journey.

She sat back on the bed and turned on the television. After flipping through the channels over the next couple of minutes and not finding anything of interest to watch, she turned the television off and threw the remote on top of the bed.

On top of the dresser lay her iPod. She decided that music would get her going because she was still moving in slow-motion. When she reached to pick up the iPod, she could see the bedroom window through the mirror atop the dresser. When she noticed how her dead husband had a blank stare that was so vacuous, not only did she scream to the top of her lungs, but she went racing throughout the house to find someplace to hide.

After checking the time on her watch, Rosa could not believe that she was hiding under the kitchen sink for nearly four hours. Time was supposed to fly by when you were having fun, not when you were terrified. Her thirty-nine-year-old body was aching after being in a fetal position for so long. She couldn't believe she was doing this after all of the early morning's activities were dedicated to bringing Warren back. But that blank look on his face just terrified the crap out of her.

The entire time while under the sink she remained as quiet and as motionless as possible, mainly to hear any sound or movement inside the entire house. Now that she could not recall hearing anything except her panicky breathing, the conclusion was that he was still outside the bedroom window.

Of all the strange things that could happen, her stomach began to growl loudly; she hadn't eaten anything since this morning. She was so excited about paying a visit to see the magic worker and later hurrying to the gravesite, all she had for nutrition up until this point was the light breakfast.

Now a loud *Bang! Bang!* The sound raced from the bedroom window, as if someone was using a closed fist to break in. The blinds rattled loudly, and it also sounded as if glass was broken.

She yelped under the sink, but quickly covered her mouth. Her heart almost jumped out of her chest. Cold ice water seemed to be pumping through her veins.

A few moments later she could hear the sound of a foot dragging across the carpet in the hallway and onto the tile in the kitchen; the sound was immediately followed by an awful aroma of dead flesh and moist dirt.

Everything all of a sudden went very quiet, but the smells were still present. Rosa opened the cabinet door to take a peek. What she saw was her dead husband looking at her with that blank stare written across his face. She quickly let the cabinet door shut, not knowing what to do next with this front-row seat of horror.

She peeked through the cabinet door again. Warren was just standing in the same position as before, both arms swinging loosely on either side, blankly staring into her direction. This time when she let the door shut she had to cover her nose as well as her mouth; he now stank badly, and she didn't want to throw up, something she was trying to avoid since this morning. Her knee tapped a large bottle of Pine-Sol, and she couldn't wait to give someone a nice hot bath filled with the cleaning liquid.

The very next day, Warren sat in his favorite chair on the front lawn. His aroma was much improved with the hot bath and a new set of clothes. Rosa may have been scared to death to get near him at first, but she realized that he didn't want to cause any harm, at least not as far as she could see at the present moment. Besides, the stink coming off his body was unbearable at first.

However, animals tend to act different in most cases than humans. The neighborhood dogs barked ferociously at him, probably because they tend to pick up scents from far away, and they probably thought Warren was dead. Vultures began to fly out of nowhere in search of a meal to scavenge for.

Warren paid no attention to the animalistic behaviors surrounding him.

Relatives began to come over after Rosa made numerous phone calls explaining to them that she had a gigantic surprise awaiting all of them. But not everyone is ready to accept every gigantic surprise thrown at them, at least not family.

The adults were all wide-eyed and wide-mouthed in surprise, knowing that four days ago a burial of this man had taken place.

The teenagers were too busy texting on their cell phones.

But sometimes there's not too much anyone can do to shut up those in the kids' category. Sometimes kids make the most off-the-top-of-the-head comments, normally with an adult screaming at them to be quiet, and they had plenty to say about Warren.

"Why is his face so blue?"

"Ooh! He's got flies buzzing all around him!"

"His fingernails look dirty!"

"Why is he just staring into space like that?"

Rosa wanted to smack every kid in her presence dead in the center of their mouth. Only she didn't want the situation against her husband to get any worse. *Maybe I'll just skip lunch and make them hungry*, she thought with a sense of silliness.

What she didn't realize was that the adults had relocated into the house and were in the living room whispering about her husband. Their comments were much worse than what the kids were saying. Especially since grown folks know how to gossip more professionally than any youngster could ever imagine. Adults know how to whisper so skillfully behind someone's back, gaining so much experience after many years of practicing the craft.

Hours after the relatives scattered away in the same direction—now the gossiping could *really* begin—Rosa tried desperately to get Warren to open his mouth and eat, but he showed no interest in the food in front of his face. She was only trying to make him happy, before *and* after his death.

The love for him was so great she comically whispered into his ear an old phrase used many times before when she said, "I would run through a lion's den with steak drawers on if that's what you want me to do to make you happy!" She blushed from cheek-to-cheek after the comment.

She pulled one of the lawn chairs up beside him and sat down, admiring his blank presence. One thing she admired about him the most now was all she needed to do was point into the direction she wanted Warren to walk, and he would obey to this command as if his brain was programmed, something a few women wish they could do to the man in their life.

She also admired the stiffness of his body, which in a strange type of way made him seem strong to her. His entire body was stiff—which caused him to sit awkwardly—even the private parts; how he was able to move around never crossed her thoughts. But the thought of making love to him crept into her mind, even with that vague look winning over his personality. Even though his odor was still strong enough to attract flies, she still could not contain herself from wanting to spend time in bed with him. She counterplanned by thinking, *Well, he does go where I tell him to! Why not point him toward the bedroom?*

She motioned with her right hand stretched out toward the door.

He immediately got up and headed in that direction, his right leg dragging up the front steps, the left leg not too far behind.

She motioned again with that same hand into the direction of the bedroom.

He continued walking, heading toward the bedroom.

She followed closely behind, still blushing from cheek-to-cheek, but this time with a little more spice, showing all her pretty white teeth.

He stood by the bedside, as if waiting for the next command.

Behind him, she began to undress.

After she was naked, she undressed Warren, ignoring the tiny maggots crawling around his privacy area; the maggots were crawling over each other as well , as if they also wanted a moment of intimacy, perhaps to secure the development of a new generation of flies to bug the crap out of the human and animal populations.

A few moments later, their bare-naked bodies lay close together, his privacy inside of hers. Since he was in a stupor, and remained motionless, she had no problem taking over the sexual encounter. Warren was normally the aggressor when it came time to lure her by acting chummy and buying her high-end gifts; it was not like he didn't want to be kind unless he simply wanted some play time. He was on top of her just staring into nothing, she looking back at him straight into his eyes, wondering if anything was able to penetrate through his mind the way he was penetrating inside her now, images in her mind of the last time they had lay together. Then, she began to form in her mind how great the sex was the first time he made love to her, particularly how when he began to release inside of her. His body excreted what seemed like nearly a pint of moisture inside her warm body, causing him to almost slip over top of her, which probably would have landed him hard onto the floor, which meant that she would've probably been caught having sex as a young girl late one night while her parents slept in the bedroom adjacent to hers. It was just so romantic to her how he had crawled inside her bedroom window one late rainy night. One of the immediate thoughts that crossed her mind as soon as he died was how great they had just made love a couple of days ago, and how much she would miss those remarkable sexual encounters; if only she could become gravid at the present moment; she had already begun to schedule their next private session.

But something strange began to happen inside of Warren's mind that Rosa was not prepared for. When he *did* manage to move his stiff body, his mouth opened widely, showcasing a nutrient-starved set of teeth, tongue, and jaws; strangely to her, the sex became much better. The odors from his mouth smelled of rot and long-ago death. His mouth went straight for Rosa's neck; she actually thought he was about to put a red mark of passion just below her earlobe. But she quickly realized that he was *biting* her. His action caused a sudden disturbance of emotions inside her mind that sped so fast she didn't even have time to sort things out into a sense of understanding. She could feel the warmth of blood trickling down her neck and inside his mouth. All day long she had been trying to feed him, trying to make his resurfacing a nice and pleasant one. But what he wanted all along was a fresh supply of meat and warm blood. She didn't even scream or seem dissatisfied as he chewed loudly on her neck, the horrible sound easy to distinguish inside the quiet bedroom. She didn't even try to escape because of the love she has for her husband.

Rosa managed one last thought while her semi-dead husband was inside of her with his stiff erection and the enormous amount of blood being lost made her want to faint: as his biting became more of a jaw-snapping affair, and his chewing was so intense that neck muscles, soft skin, and warm blood slipped inside his mouth, she finally stopped imagining how great a love-maker Warren actually was. Instead, she hated herself for prying into other folks business and overhearing the conversation of who the magic worker was and where he lived.

At Nighttime

When nighttime comes, things would get worse for Jeremy. Every night brought on the same nightmarish thoughts of wanting daylight to arrive fast, to see the giant yellow star rise over the eastern horizon.

He began to have these thoughts of evil spirits chasing after him shortly after his family moved from a trailer park to a large apartment complex on the other side of town. The thoughts always repulsed him. He just couldn't understand as a teenager why he was so afraid of the dark now but was okay with it as a young boy. He would think, *Maybe something evil happened in this unit.*

Jeremy was a well-liked kid in the neighborhood, even though he didn't grow up with most of the teenagers in the development. Any time a team would be picked—normally basketball, football, or baseball—his name would be selected either first or second, no matter *who* was picking the teams. Even the young ladies liked him a lot; they would tell him all the time how attractive he was, and he got a lot of phone numbers. And even when they played hide-and-seek, at least two of the young ladies made sure to get caught, preferably behind one of the apartment buildings out of sight from snoopy eyes. But no one in the neighborhood knew how much he feared the nighttime.

The day was one Thursday, around eight o'clock, when things became worst. The sun was about to set on this late September evening. He started to get extremely nervous, knowing that soon it would be dark; it would also be time to go inside, eat dinner, watch some television, and get ready for bed.

By 11:00 p.m., he was still awake in his bedroom listening to music. A small lamp glowed in the corner of his bedroom near the entrance, emitting enough light to keep his room from becoming completely dark; the lamp could easily be turned on or off if he just went to the edge of the opposite sleeping side of his bed.

Suddenly, a loud knock banged on his bedroom door.

"Come in," he spoke softly.

"Hi, Jeremy," spoke his dwarf sister Lucinda. "Did you get enough to eat? I'm asking because Mom just put the leftovers into the refrigerator."

"I'm good, little sis."

"Okay. Well, just in case you get hungry later, everything will be in the blue Tupperware containers on the top shelf," she informed in her high-pitched squeaky voice.

"Thanks, sis. Now you go to bed, okay. It's getting way past your bedtime."

"Okay."

One of the reasons Jeremy was afraid of the dark—even though he didn't realize it yet—was contributed by seeing so many horror movies; he started thinking they were real. Even seeing the first commercials for the upcoming Halloween season frightened him. It was just before bedtime one night when he was winding down and about to get ready for bed. The commercial that flashed across the television screen advertised that a man who had knives for fingers while at the same time wearing a mask was going to stalk all the babysitters at a camp called Crystal Lake that was adjacent to a corn field that had numerous small infants roaming the streets singing baleful words just off the top of their heads. For the most part, he was not at the age to realize that the commercials are always better than the actual film, in any genre.

At 11:30 p.m., the small beam of light was off. But he still had the radio on; listening to music gave him assistance to think of other matters besides the demons, who would inevitably torture his inner spirit. The radio station on the air had a special late-night guest for its late-night talk show host. The guest—a ghost hunter who wanted to be known by the listening audience as The Ghost Huntsman, who unknowingly was a friend of Jeremy's mother—discussed in particular of how to rid a dwelling of ghosts, no matter the number. The Ghost Huntsman explained that if you felt the presence of a demonic spirit inside a dwelling, the way you could keep them from bothering you was to plaster newspaper articles all over your walls to occupy the spirits by forcing them to read.

Jeremy never thought of the idea that a ghost or spirit could actually live in a dwelling. Now he was more terrified in the darkness than ever before, especially since the talk show's host was normally someone interested in music.

His fear of spirits was enhanced when he overhead his friends talking about how if you slept on your stomach, the devil could get a free ride on your back. The more tired you felt after awakening, the longer the duration of Satan's ride.

Close to three the next morning Jeremy woke up. The radio station surprisingly still had the same guest talking on the radio station, but this time he was yelling out loud and speaking in tongues, as if he were possessed by some sort of demonic spirit.

Jeremy got out of bed and turned the radio off, his legs wobbly from fear. Next, he walked into the living room and gathered a few newspapers out of the paper rack near the front door. He remembered that a roll of duct tape was always kept in the top drawer closest to the stove in the kitchen. An hour later, newspapers were taped across all four corners of his bedroom, which included the window but not the entrance door. He managed to sleep well the next few hours before daybreak.

Later that morning, his mother awoke him for breakfast and school. After turning on the overhead light she shouted, "Why in the heck do you have all these newspapers taped up on my walls! This is about the weirdest thing I've ever seen you do, Jeremy!"

He felt that it was time to face his fears like a man and stop holding subjects that bothered him inside. "I taped them up to keep some spirits from haunting me. A man named the Ghost Huntsman said it was a good idea late last night on the radio."

His mother only shook her head in disbelief, never mentioning that she knew the ghost hunter, knowing that only small children should be afraid of this nonsense. "You have twenty minutes, young man, to be at the table for breakfast, or I'm going to take—" She stopped for a moment as if to not make matters worse than what they already were, especially since kids were already so disrespectful to their parents nowadays. Because deep down inside she knew that spirits of some kind roamed all over the earth. All she could do at this moment was hope and pray that her son would not be overtaken by something not of this world. If only his father was here...

Jeremy didn't feel ashamed after talking to his mother this morning, nor did he feel ashamed when a few of the neighborhood kids stopped by his house to see if he wanted to play some kickball after school. He was already prepared for the rest of the kids to pick on him by making the *woo* sound that ghosts are supposed to make, because he knew that kids gossip just as much as adults, especially about something of this nature.

After school, he came straight home and lay flat on his back in bed. He only thought of putting today's paper on the uncovered ceiling. The room was close to being dark, and he began to get sleepy; he slept for over an hour.

While he slept peaceably, his room became quite chilly as he began to dream about things he saw during the day. The creatures that crawled out of his closet and budged around and under his bed were as small as a pygmy rabbit, but they were as ugly as a blob fish, and about as slimy as well. They left trails of snot and sticky moisture on everything that they touched. By the time they finished crawling over the walls and ceiling, the trail left behind smudged the writings on the newspapers.

It was good the creatures didn't awake him. If he would've seen them and their ugly appearance, he would've either slept outside the apartment's front door, or found another place of rest over any one of his many friends' apartments. But strangely, part of what his vivid dream was about was how earlier in the day he and a group of friends smashed a few slimy snails that crawled from under the ground after a recent storm; he could even smell the rotted moisture of the dead tree even in his dream.

A hand suddenly burst through the paper covering the window. That scared the living crap out of Jeremy. He was also angry as the paper covering the window ripped to pieces.

When he turned on the small lamp in the corner near the door, he freaked out at seeing the trails of moisture covering the papers, and the sticky wetness over his bed sheets, pillow, and the hardwood floor.

Outside the window, he was disgusted at hearing a group of kids either laughing or *wooing* loudly at him. One of them could be seen trying to shake the unknown slimy substance off their hand.

He got up and flicked on the overhead light, the bedroom now in full glow, an angry frown covering his face. He then grabbed the tape and pieced the newspaper back together as best he could. He wasn't even hungry after smelling the aroma of chicken coming from the kitchen. He decided to just go back to bed to catch up on lost sleep.

The next day, Jeremy got up bright and early, intent on enjoying another warm late-summer day. He sat up in bed shortly after awakening. He noticed that every single page of newspaper was vacated from the walls, including the torn pages from the window that he carefully taped back together earlier. He had no idea which direction to go into next. Asking his small sister would be ridiculous. He knew not to ask his mother because she only came into his room to wake him when her very firm week-day early morning knocks were unsuccessful. But he still wanted answers.

The phone began to ring in the living room. He over-heard his mother answer it. A short time later, his mother was sobbing and screaming into the phone, "You're kid-ding me!"

Jeremy knew something bad had happened from the tone of his mother's voice.

"How in God's name did that happen? I've known him for so many years, and that's all he wanted to do in life!"

Jeremy continued to listen, praying inside his mind that nothing terrible had happened to someone close to him.

Lucinda burst open Jeremy's bedroom door, hold-ing tightly on to the doorknob to avoid falling on the floor. In a childish voice she explained, "Mommy said the Ghost Huntsman is dead. Who is the Ghost Huntsman, Jeremy?"

The news of the Ghost Huntsman's death spread quickly, being covered by every local radio station and television show, probably because he died in such an unfa-miliar way. Newscasters reported that the man known for hunting ghosts and solving cases dealing with demonic spirits died with large bundles of slimy newspapers stuffed down his throat, with his mouth and nose covered tightly with nearly a half roll of duct tape. Authorities figured that the rest of the roll of duct tape was used to tightly secure the victim's hands behind his back.

All day Jeremy walked the hallways at school baffled. All he wanted to do was face up to his fears and become a mature young man, and now this happens.

At nighttime, he lay on his bed staring at the ceiling, at the same time listening to the radio. He wanted to make a call to the station to offer his condolences. Up to this point in his life, it was the only station he enjoyed listening to, but since the killer was said to be on the loose, he didn't want to be questioned about anything.

He also knew that whatever happened in his room last night had never happened before, until he heard of the special guest on the radio last night. With the Ghost Huntsman now dead, he wondered if the strangeness would occur again, or phase out with the ghost hunter's death.

"Hello out there! This is Deejay Doctor Spin playing all the hits you need to get through the night! What song would you like to hear? Give us a call at 1-800-492-WHNC! Hurry up and call because we have a special guest coming up in just a few moments! The Ghost Huntsman is his name, and freeing your house of evil spirits is his game!"

That last statement left Jeremy in a state of disarray. He knew that if the ghost hunter was somehow not dead, there was no telling what strangeness would take place in his bedroom tonight; last night's dream still had a lasting impression in his mind. He wondered if anyone else listening to this same station had the same happenings last night also, because the station was very popular in town and had many listeners. No way he was the only one, or he was the only one afraid of the dark and this *didn't* happen to anyone else. But he still had enough sense to know that this would be the last night that he would ever listen to Doctor Spin's radio show, or any other deejay whose name began with the word *doctor*.

The Witch That Won't Leave Me Alone

Father and Mother were sure to get me up every Sunday morning, *very* early, to get ready for church. Nothing in this world ever mattered on Sunday but church. To top it off, the services would normally last all day, which meant a shortened weekend for a teenager.

But over the years, after living on my own, I came to love going to church, so much that I became a priest. A priest not only well-respected in my congregation but to all my peers in close proximity.

Over those years, I've lectured to many thousands of worshippers from all parts of the country. The respect for me had grown to the point that newer priests near and far were sent to me to job shadow my skills.

Until I joined a vigilante of priests who took their religious beliefs to an extreme measure where the main focus was catching witches, and going by any means to end the life of those, from what they expressed to me as part of my initiation, "those that practice evil must die!"

Which brings me to this point.

There's a witch that won't leave me alone, because one day years ago while on a trail to catch a witch with a group of these same priests mentioned earlier, in the middle of the day we caught one, bound her arms tightly behind her back, and sat her on a horse. The inside scoop we received let us write to her, and she wasn't surprised at all when she was found, somehow seemingly accepting what she knew we were about to do to her. Moments later after being on horseback, she was carried and placed right under the noose that was skillfully knotted that would be used to doom her life. But just before the ritual was complete, we locked eyes.

No surprises there because all witches have to be killed.

That was my first trial—and my last, I may add—to catch a witch. I was told by group of priests that the first one is always the roughest, but soon you will get over it and be quickly ready for the next trial.

The sad part is I don't think I ever will get over it. The way her head flopped around the rope and the slight breeze that made her dark attire flutter around her now cold frame was something I now know I wasn't prepared for.

But now, after all these years that have zipped away,

anytime I'm attracted to a woman and get close to her, I see the witch's face, mostly when it's time to get intimate. For one, as a priest I shouldn't be out looking for women, except for the one I will plan to marry. And two, I somehow feel that this particular witch is the most beautiful woman I had ever seen in my life!

After devoting my life away from heathen pleasures and getting back to worshipping with all my heart and soul, everything was fine and dandy.

Until recently.

A month ago, there was a tapping on my bedroom window during a stormy night. At first, I thought the sound came from the branches on a few trees near the window that made the noises like on any other stormy night. But when this storm passed, while at the same time the wind ceased, the tapping continued. The only other sound was my heavy breathing as my heart pulsed harder.

An hour later, the noises became more ear-splitting. I wanted to desperately go to the window to see what was *really* going on, which at that late hour puzzled me.

Despite the noises and my fear of them, I dozed off to sleep anyway. But with the bright star rising high in the sky that morning, the noises continued. The only thing left for me to do was get out of bed and go to investigate this strange occurrence. When I opened the blinds and looked out, I didn't see a person, but the trees closest to my bedroom window were draped in black cloth.

I love you with all my heart.

When I heard those words coming from a place I couldn't quite point out I almost panicked. But I needed to keep my thoughts and sanity intact and on one accord. After shutting my eyes tightly and opening them again, outside my bedroom window the black sheets had somehow disappeared from covering the trees.

I quickly tried to erase my thoughts from what I just heard whispered and the sight outside the window, but for hours they were both recited over and over again in my mind.

Later that day, I paid a visit to my church home, went inside as fast as I could, and kneeled by the altar. I just didn't know exactly what type of prayer requests I wanted to make.

That night right before bed, while undressing, I had the feeling that something was going to happen again. And it did. An hour after lying in bed unable to sleep, there was that same tapping, but this time, the sound came downstairs from the front door. I began praying as loud as I could, but the tapping became as loud as I prayed, drowning out my words.

I stomped to the front door, sort of knowing that I would see something that would seem unbelievable. When I opened the door and the numerous black sheets smashed me dead in the face, almost knocking my frame backward, it was certified in stone right then that my days of trailing witches were over; I kind of felt that way back then.

I will never leave you alone!

Just the other day I had the deepest desire to hang myself, and this morning to just drink a bottle of poison, to be in eternity forever with the witch that wouldn't leave me alone. Every time I stepped outside after the visit to my church home, the smoldering heap of black smoke that was getting energy from I don't know where and racing up and down the neighboring streets would give anyone the thoughts of killing themselves. And the farther I stepped away from the front porch, that same black smoke rushed into my direction, raising high as if to come down atop my head, while at the same time distorting my vision. Because if I continued to live, she would continue to show up in some way, shape, or form, which meant that my faith was not as concrete as I thought it was.

Author's Note

An array of thoughts float through the minds of all of us. But to put those thoughts down on paper is a totally different ball game.

It's called being a writer, or the individual who *knows* how to put their thoughts down for others to read. And those who tend to pursue this mental happiness can get joy out of perfecting their craft, which can take them above the highest clouds in the sky.

The thoughts that floated through my mind while writing these stories in this collection are some that I'm very proud of, and some that I'm not. I've decided that you as the reader can categorize each one for yourself.

I hope you enjoy every single one of them; may you have at least one nightmare or possibly more. And remember, if writing is a dream you want to accomplish, keep those thoughts floating, and keep putting them down in print for the world to one day read.